For [illegible]
Regards

Death by Suicidal Means

From [illegible]

Death by Suicidal Means

Walter
Henderson

The Killing of Wardell Burge

CHAPEL HILL, NC USA

Inheritance Press,Inc., Chapel Hill 27514

Library of Congress Catalog Card Number: 93-061056
HARDCOVER:
ISBN 0-9638086-0-5
PAPER TRADE:
ISBN 0-9638086-1-3

Preface

Some laws are inherently wrong. One such law is the outlawry statute. Employing the outlawry statute is an endorsement of barbarism which should not be tolerated in modern society. Outlawry places an individual outside the protection of the law. In various forms it dates to A.D. 600. By the thirteenth century any person declared an outlaw was put to death without trial.

North Carolina first embraced the concept of outlawry in 1741 to bring in runaway slaves. It was used on occasion in the eighteenth and early nineteenth centuries in Pennsylvania and Virginia. Outlawry was employed infrequently except in North Carolina, fell into disuse in state courts, and was unknown in federal law. The North Carolina outlawry statute in its present form was declared unconstitutional in 1976. It has never been purged from the state's general statutes. As long as it remains law, we face the possibility of outlawry proclamations being initiated by any citizen out of malice or ignorance.

Death by Suicidal Means concerns the tragic results of an outlawry proclamation issued against James Wardell Burge, a mentally ill black man. I hope this book pricks the social conscience of Americans today and creates a public outcry for the removal of these outmoded laws.

WALTER HENDERSON

...any citizen may slay him without accusation of any crime.[1]

...the fire started after a posse...hurled tear gas into the second story room.[2]

... deceased came to his death by suicidal means and was directly due to asphyxiation and burning and that no criminal act or default was involved.[3]

---

1 NCGS 15-48 declared unconstitutional. See Appendix A

2 Newspaper Articles Covering Burge's Death. See Appendix B

3 Verdict of Coroner's Jury filed 7-1-65, Jones County Superior Court, Trenton, N.C.

Al Jackson

On a rain-blotched day in May in the belly of piney-woods eastern North Carolina, three men, haunted by heat dogs, and acting under the authority of an outlawry proclamation, pushed a sheriff's cruiser along a blacktop county road. They were on a mission to bring in Wardell Burge, dead or alive.

They were not pushing the car because of mechanical failure. They were using it as a shield, a moving bulwark, to protect them from the fire of the twenty-two caliber rifle they thought Wardell Burge would use. That was the district attorney's idea. It would be too dangerous to have a driver. He would be in the direct line of fire.

Sheriff Tate, gunless, dressed in a black suit and felt

hat, limped behind. Wearing military fatigues, the men were pushing against the trunk and fenders with their left hands. Two carried twelve-gauge shotguns and the other carried a thirty-ought-six rifle slung over his shoulder.

Their heads tilted upward, their eyes angled sharply across the top of the cruiser toward a two-story frame house. The house stood in a curve a half-mile down the asphalt road. Sporadic clouds, lead-bellied with silver linings, sped overhead.

Deputy Al Jackson pushed strenuously beside the district attorney. His thick hips churned his force down his legs. He wore a gun belt fitted tightly around his waist. It held three loaded magazines for his three-fifty-seven magnum pistol, an electrical shocking device the size of a man's wallet, five double-ought buckshot shells, two pairs of handcuffs, a can of mace, two billy sticks, one eighteen inches and one ten inches, and an incendiary round for his shotgun.

A small windswept cloud passed and squirted on them.

"Blue skies, smilin' at me, nothin' but blue skies do I see," Al sang, and grunted a laugh.

In North Carolina, April showers come in May. Clouds cluster like giant cotton balls mixing and intermixing until the showers come as softly and gently as tiny strings of cotton. Sometimes a shower falls on one side of the highway while the sun shines on the other.

Nature walks through time zones as if her personality is splitting up, dividing moisture into air and air into moisture. Light into shadow and shadow into light. Clouds pass in erratic paths, some squirting bursts of rain and others passing as if in jest. Strings of flashing silver sporadically mix with the pure clear sunlight.

The sun sparkled as if shining through water.

Al Jackson loved his work. He told his fellow officers he had rather beat a man than kill him. When you kill a person, it terminates the relationship. You lose that flesh to flesh contact. Lose that violent flesh to flesh contact that makes you feel free. This feeling gives a continuing sense of power as long as the man can live and take it. Of course there were situations where you had to kill people. He felt he would like that too.

When Al learned from the sheriff that the district attorney had obtained an outlawry proclamation against Wardell Burge, his belly tightened. His teeth grated. His heart beat fast and strong and his eyes blinked.

He would get that damn nigger. Crazy or not, nobody, more especially a damn nigger, had the right to walk the roads naked with a gun. He didn't have the right to take over a church, even if it was a nigger church, and preach to them while he was naked as a jaybird. Wardell being a nigger made it ten times worse, and ten times easier to do the job.

Jackson had enormous, clumsy strength. His shoulders were narrower than his hips. His waist was thick and tapered toward his shoulders. He leaned forward whether walking or standing. Al's walk was ponderous and powerful. His arms hung like angle iron and did not move at the elbows when he walked. He always wore a military cap pulled down, so that the rim of the hat fitted across eyebrows that bristled like briars over dusty, grey eyes fixed in an unfaltering gaze.

When called in on a domestic dispute, Al pulled his hat a little further down, tightened the muscles on his face, narrowed his eyes, settled back in his cruiser and made his call.

His first move upon entering the house was to grab the husband, who was drunk most of the time, and methodically thump him around. He always smiled when he did that, raised his lips to show his teeth, like a dog before attacking. Al liked the feeling and went about it as if roping a calf. There was a pleasure he did not understand after the licks passed and the drunk husband lay cowering at his feet. It was like sex, which he thought he loved, although he did not understand it.

"Come at once!" Amy Killingsworth had called him a year ago, "come at once!"

Al knew her situation. She was in a second marriage to a naval veteran who was on medical retirement. Amy had seen Al in the courthouse occasionally when she was paying taxes or taking care of other business. They passed compatible glances. She mentioned that she and Robert argued, sometimes heatedly, but said he'd never hit her. Robert was very emotional and excitable, and

Amy said, unpredictable. And he liked guns.

When Al arrived, Robert was not there. Amy sat quietly on the couch. Al looked into her black eyes. He had drawn his short billy club and was tapping it in a slow measured rhythm in the palm of his hand.

"What's the matter?" he asked. He sat cautiously next to her and continued tapping his hand with his billy club.

Al liked to counsel battered women. Sometimes he would spend considerable time telling them he was their protector, that he was always on call to come to their rescue, and any time they needed him, they should call.

Albert Jackson never struck his wife. Their arguments were resolved with a firm, "Now you can't do that," or "no we are going to do it this way." He never wanted to strike her. Yet he relished pounding on men. He did not understand that about himself and rarely thought about it. Pounding men at his mercy was like the power of a steam engine rushing through him. Al quickly dispatched any concern for his actions with an interior smile.

"It's Robert. He's gone. Bought him a house trailer and moved in it. It's about five miles down the road on the Wilcox place."

"Are you scared of him?" Al asked calmly as he sheathed the club and squinted at her.

"No. He's never beat on me. He's got those mental problems he had when he was in the Navy. He cries and hollers a lot."

Al peered at her from beneath the rim of his cap. "What do you want me to do?" He pulled the barrel of his pistol off the couch and twisted his hips for more comfort.

Amy Killingsworth lay her chubby hand softly on Al's thigh. He felt the warm, moist hand and suddenly it became a part of him. A spasm ran through him, yet nothing about him moved. Her auburn hair twirled up in a loose bun above her ear where tiny beads of perspiration glowed.

"You know," she said in a flat monotone. Her eyes bulged fiercely at him as if there were enormous pressure inside her and all of it centered in her eyes.

"He ain't had sex with me in five years. Sometimes I think I'm going crazy. Sometimes I think it's me that's crazy."

He studied her a moment, twitching the corners of his mouth. Was he lucky or simply powerful in looks?

"We don't want you to go crazy," he said as he stood and unbuckled his gun belt. Her eyes followed his motions, like two black magnets following a piece of iron.

Al's Toll

"Let's stop here a minute boys and see what the weather's going to do," the sheriff said as he turned and pulled a bottle of Little Brown Jug from his inner coat pocket and took a drink.

"Right there's where Burge preached," he said and nodded toward the church to their left. He gazed at the church as if musing over a nemesis.

A bluebird perched in the crape myrtle bush alongside the road and began singing.

The three men straightened up and looked at the church suspiciously as if suddenly it had become an adversary. Al Jackson walked over to the bell, which sat on a platform in front of the church, and pulled the hammer. A clear toll shot down the road.

"Wonder if he can hear that?" he questioned.

"Leave the bell alone," the sheriff said.

The men looked uneasily down the road at the white framed two-story house and walked back to the rear of the cruiser and began pushing. The sheriff continued limping behind them.

The small, weather-worn frame church was built by John Burge in 1868. The bell, mounted on a brick platform beneath the myrtle, was placed there after the Klan fired the church and damaged the vestry in 1900. The huge bell arrived by train from Massachusetts in 1875. "P. R." was engraved inside the bell jar.

After the fire, the congregation decided to leave the bell mounted in front of the church. They rigged a hammerhead to bang the side of the bell from the inside without the bell moving. It was a clumsy fixture shaped like an elbow anchored below the bell on the platform. The hammerhead extended into the mouth of the bell and could be activated by the arm on the outside.

After the Civil War, John Burge, grandfather to Wardell, acquired land in a swampy, desolate area of Ownes County and established a church on the stretch of road known as the Catfish Lake Road. He named it Myrtle Grove First United Church of Christ. His family and the black community of that area attended the church.

The sanctuary contained unpainted hand-hewn pine

benches. The pulpit had three oak chairs, plainly decorated, and behind the chairs was the choir section, which consisted of three pine benches. On the wall behind the choir was a large tapestry of the Last Supper, the only decoration in the church. A small pine pulpit lectern stood in front of the choir section.

This is where Wardell Burge preached, naked.

Greg Butler

Al pushed beside the district attorney and continued to hum "blue skies, dah da dee." He gazed up the road at the home of Wardell Burge.

Pushing beside him, the others grunted occasionally and wiped the rain and sweat from their brow. Greg Butler, the sniper, was on special assignment from the State Bureau of Investigation.

Greg's face was square. His crew cut made his head appear as if hewn from a block of wood. He was clean shaven at all times and wore Aqua Velva which gave his face the glow of a boy and the sweet smell of a woman. His cobalt blue eyes sliced from side to side, glinting with the insensitive force of a butcher. His eyes were as callous and expressionless as the hunter's knife as it draws breath from the beast and lets its entrails. Without feeling, as when taking a shower, singing in monotones.

He was happily married with two children: a girl, age six and a boy, age ten. He was a conservative, a Baptist, and a Sunday school teacher who loved his work. The Old Testament provided his sense of justice. Greg believed God was a wrathful God who meted out justice swift and certain, without emotion or feeling for the sinner or lawbreaker. Justice was the bulwark that kept wrong from invading the province of good. God and His teachings were right and the devil and his doings were wrong. Greg wanted to be on the firing line, in swift pursuit of the lawbreaker, and known as a protector of the American way.

He had worked up to second in command on the SWAT Team. When Luke Hampton contacted Rufus Winston, Director of the SBI, concerning Burge, Greg volunteered his services. Rufus often used him to bring in dangerous criminals who had escaped Central Prison.

He was married to Ethel Wineberry, a blue-eyed woman from Johnston County who went to community college and studied accounting. They met at Clayton High School. Greg was a senior in high school when his father died.

Greg had rigid rules for his wife and children. No television nor movies unless Christian-oriented. He loved his children in his protective way, but showed no emotion to them. Greg lived in a vacuum and his communications to his family were like static discharges neutralizing opposite polarities, like lightning leaping from cloud to cloud, sky to earth.

Greg Butler was one-quarter Indian and a quiet family man. As a boy he had worked in his father's feed mill and played on the Clayton football team. He turned down an athletic scholarship to pursue criminal justice at the community college.

His father, a lay preacher in the Baptist church, accepted the Bible as the Book from God—unalterable, untouchable and the exact words to follow.

He had never killed a man. Never shot a man. Although he had seen a dead man, he had never seen one die.

"Ethel," he said over his ham and eggs, "I'm going to be on a posse over in Ownes County next week. Luke Hampton, the district attorney in the fourth district asked Rufus if he would send me."

Her first love was for her children and Greg. She feared for Greg's life because of his work. She was apprehensive about his putting his life in jeopardy to capture criminals. She hoped someday he could do something else. That was his decision to make.

Ethel was tentative. She had seen Greg leave on several missions to capture escaped murderers from Central Prison. It was no heroic thing to her. She remembered too well, after his first year on the SWAT Team, the night he said, "we lost Gene Riggs today."

He waited until Greg Jr. had gone to bed before telling the story. She knew something was wrong. He was restless and secretive and his eyes diverted from her repeatedly.

"How?" Ethel asked.

"From ambush. Up there at the head of White Oak River. We were staked out for James Kornegay and Brent Hill. They broke out of Central last week, you know, and worked their way down there in the pocosin. Gene was staked in the thickest part and James got in behind him and slit his throat. That's the way things happen. It was just his time."

The words bounced back and forth in his mind. He did not believe them. They were hollow, filling the vacuum that he was coming to believe he carried with him. It was a distant thought like something was trying to tell him that man had no choices.

Greg wanted everything to stop when he found Gene. Evil had plucked the life out of good. He looked into Gene's lifeless eyes and knew that Gene had stopped. Maybe it was God's strange way.

Was God dictating every little thing, including man's choices? It was disturbing.

He pushed his plate away, looked at Ethel and added, "I'm the one who found him."

"What's going on over there in Ownes County?" Ethel asked.

"A crazy man is terrorizing the community. He walks the highway naked and takes over his church and preaches naked. People are up in arms about it. They got an outlawry proclamation against him. They say that means he can be brought in dead or alive."

"Be careful," Ethel uttered her concern.

"I will," he answered.

Luke's Law

"Hold up boys," the district attorney said. He stopped pushing, stood up and wiped the sweat from his face.

"Take a look, Greg, and see what'cha can see."

The men stopped. Greg laid his rifle against the cruiser and pulled his binoculars from the case on his belt. He focused on the house in the curve.

Luke Hampton, the district attorney, was a pudgy man with tight, firm jowls, giving his face the appearance of a hog with a short nose. He was cheerful and humorous and in his spare time he was either reading the latest state court appellate decisions, classical literature, or having a glass of bourbon. For Luke, quotes from Shakespeare, the Bible, Homer, Socrates, Plato, Omar

Khayyam or Kahlil Gibran came as easily as the general statues of North Carolina.

Luke pushed from the right fender of the cruiser, the most vulnerable position to the gunfire expected from Wardell Burge. He carried a twelve-gauge shotgun. If necessary, he would lead the charge of the posse to bring in Wardell Burge. He told the sheriff a year ago that he planned to run for governor or supreme court justice and he wanted to do something spectacular. To get his adrenaline flowing.

That is the reason he had the outlawry proclamation in his shirt pocket.

The sheriff called the district attorney's office about his problem.

"Got your call, Sheriff. What kind of problem you got?" Luke asked as he pulled a chair up to the sheriff's desk.

He drove from Carteret County at the sheriff's request. Luke was told it was urgent and could not be discussed over the phone.

The sheriff reached in his bottom desk drawer and pulled out a bottle of Little Brown Jug and two small cups. He poured the cups half-full and finished filling them with Coca-Cola, then handed the district attorney a cup and drank from the other.

"We've got a real problem with a colored man. A real problem, Luke."

He paused and looked the district attorney in the eye.

The sheriff's eyes were brown and glassy. His head, which seemed fatter than the other parts of his body, sat sideways as if it were a clay figure the potter had not finished.

Sheriff Tate had the reputation as the best deputy in the history of Ownes County. After he became sheriff, he never carried a gun. He went gunless, he said, because guns should never be used except in bad emergencies. "I don't have them. Other law officers might but I don't."

He used what he called reason, common sense, or horse sense "which ain't nothing but stable thinkin'," he said. Patience was the most important thing a law enforcement officer had. If he had the patience to wait things out, they would usually take care of themselves. That was the trouble with most officers, they were in too big a hurry to get things done. Like yesterday. If somebody called about an assault, a family squabble or something, take your time in getting there. Like the next day or later. By the time you got there the disease would have run its course.

That's the way just about everything is. If you give it enough time it will run its course.

The Wardell Burge case was different. This was an emergency. Even at that, he reasoned, other people could carry the guns.

"Luke, this fellow named Wardell Burge has been giving us hell for over a year now. He's been in and out of mental institutions for the past five years. Come from a very intelligent colored family. His brothers and sister are teachers and doctors and things. Don't none of them live here. He lives there on the homeplace with his mama. Wardell was in the Army during World War Two and something happened to him. In 1950 he was admitted to the VA hospital in Winston-Salem and they declared him incompetent. What for I don't know. Anyhow he's been in and out of the hospital since 1950, declared competent and incompetent I don't know how many times."

The sheriff paused, tipped his cup and cleared his throat. He took his hat off and laid it on the corner of the desk. His hair was combed slick down and parted in the middle. Tiny beads of perspiration lined his forehead.

The last time Luke Hampton prosecuted in Ownes County he stood in the street at night admiring the courthouse. The fog hung on the fingers of the lights from the courthouse and the street like a van Gogh painting.

Street lights illuminated the front of the building. He liked to sit on the ledge that bordered the courthouse square and admire the justice building. Yet, as he grew into the legal profession there also grew a latent distrust for the competency of the law. Luke saw and felt the flaws of the law flowing through man's bent will and ego. He was part of the system and he would survive its edicts. He would do that. He had seen mankind, throughout history, make the law do what he wanted it to do to serve his selfish ends. He was part of that, too. It bothered him.

As he stood in front of the courthouse, the lights flooded the front of the building and gave it a ghostly look, like a face with dark gloomy eyes. The windows stared out of the depths of darkness through a brief chasm of light into the pit of darkness again. The gloom and heroics of the building moved him.

The district attorney emptied his cup.

"The real problem started," the sheriff continued, "in February, two years ago, when the veterans hospital released him as competent. He come home to stay with his mama and he started going down to his mama's church and preaching. He would just stand up in the church and preach and make the preacher stop. The congregation got scared of him and got his mama to go to the clerk of court and sign a petition to get him committed to Dorothea Dix Hospital.

"Oh yeah, he shot and killed one of his neighbor's hogs and got to carrying his rifle around. With all this stuff on the petition we had to go get him. When we went after him, I got help from the sheriff in Onslow County, had him bring his crack deputy, Alfred Revelle, you know him, to come along. Ole Wardell had holed up on the second floor of an old tenant shack down the road from his house.

"You know what? When we got there he shot one

time and Deputy Jackson put sixteen rounds of tear gas in on him and he still didn't come out. Things got quiet and the boys went in the bottom floor. They called and called for him to come down but there was no answer. Then I told them to take a chain saw and saw the floor down.

"When that floor come down, Burge come with it, with a knife in each hand. He just lay there with that idiotic look coming out of his eyes. The boys took him on up to the hospital.

"We thought that would of been the end of it but they turned him loose in sixty days. Can you imagine that? Turning a damn crazy man loose, I mean a dangerous, crazy man, on the public."

The sheriff poured more whiskey and Coca-Cola in the cups.

"But this time it's worse. Much worse. Over the past several weeks he's been walking the road between his house and the main highway, naked, with his gun. He's stopped the mail carrier three times in the month and turned her back. Can you imagine how much she was insulted and terrified?"

The district attorney's beaver-like eyes focused on the sheriff.

"Now he's taken over the Myrtle Grove Church. He goes down there and holds the congregation hostage and preaches. They don't have no air condition' in that church and sometimes he keeps them in there way past twelve into the afternoon. You can imagine what kind of scent is in there with all that heating and sweating. You sweat more and put off more body heat and a different scent when you are held at gunpoint. Several times he has run people out of their yards by walking down the road naked with his gun.

"When he starts insulting the white women the way he's doing, somethin's gotta be done. I ain't got but a deputy and a half. One full-time white deputy, Albert Jackson, and my part-time Negro, Sugar Hill. That just ain't enough to bring in Wardell. Right now traffic can't even travel from the main highway down the Catfish Lake Road."

The sheriff tipped his cup again. "You see what kind of mess I'm in. I get along good with the coloreds. But one thing is for sure, the whites ain't going to put up with a colored man parading at will up and down the public highway naked with a gun. And add to that him claimin' the road and the church."

A mood of helplessness coupled with a plea for help muted the glassy glitter in the sheriff's eyes. He looked into the district attorney's eyes and waited. It was as if Burge himself were holding him at bay.

The courthouse did not have an air conditioner. Luke loosened his tie. His red hair glistened with hair oil and stood as if fluffed. He drank from his cup then leaned forward. "There is a time and a place for all things, Sheriff," Luke said.

He paused and drank, set his cup down and fixed his eyes on the sheriff, "You can make the law do anything you want it to. I heard that from a great jurist but I won't call his name.

"What you mean by that?" the sheriff asked.

"You can get him with an outlawry proclamation," Luke said with iron in his voice. " 'Course it's been a long time since one's been used in North Carolina."

The sheriff's glassy eyes never left Luke. He did not show emotion. He had been sheriff twelve years but he had never heard of an outlawry proclamation. "What kind of thing is that?"

"It's when a person is declared an outlaw by a judge or justice. One can be issued based on a petition by a district attorney saying that a person is a felon and refuses to come in and surrender. With the outlawry proclamation, the sheriff can, if the criminal refuses to surrender after he is called to, use whatever force is necessary to bring him in. Even shooting him down on sight." Luke tipped his cup. Sweat began popping across his forehead like blisters.

"I'm gonna' hafta' get this place air conditioned," the sheriff said. "Them damn county commissioners are so dumb they don't know that justice generates heat."

Luke slackened his tie again, took another sip, smiled and said. "That's right, justice generates heat, and the courthouse generates a lot of heat."

The sheriff chuckled and said, "but that would be on

our side, I think. Ain't no jury would sit through this kind of heat without finding a man guilty."

He paused and mixed more whiskey and Coca-Cola. "How can we get one of them papers?"

"We'll have to file an affidavit with our resident superior court judge," Luke said. "I know Judge Moore real good. He's holding court in Raleigh right now. I supported him strong, and you did too, when he ran for judge. Very conservative. A strong believer in law and order. If we fill out the paper right, he'll sign it."

"Is that all there is to it?"

"We've got to show the man is involved in a lot of criminal activity and outside the control of the law. He's got to be a fugitive from justice. In effect, a wild and vicious animal. Then Judge Moore can declare him an outlaw and free him of any protection from the law. With that showing he can issue an outlawry proclamation. Something else." Luke shuffled in his seat as if gaining purchase, and continued, "You can form a posse and bring him in dead or alive." He relaxed as if he had won a murder case and the court had passed the death sentence.

"Is Wardell all that stuff you named? I mean, yeah, he's parading up and down the highway naked carrying a gun and taking over the church. Sure, there's enough. Can you fill out the papers for me?"

"Yeah. We'll fix one. The judge will sign it."

He gulped his drink and set the cup in front of the

sheriff.

"That's enough for me, Sheriff. We'll get that petition up and I'll have that paper for you next week."

"How am I going to carry this thing out?" the sheriff asked.

"Have you ever formed a posse?"

"No," the sheriff answered.

"Form one. It's easy. All you got to do is call a group of men together to search for and bring in a criminal. The outlawry proclamation will give you the authority to bring him in dead or alive."

"Who could I get?" the sheriff asked.

"Me, for one."

"Al, my deputy would be a good one. He's got guts like iron. He'll stick."

"I know a fellow on the SWAT Team. Greg Butler. He's been on several missions to bring in escapees."

"How many you reckon we need?"

"I think four of us will be enough."

"Can you contact Greg?"

"Yeah."

It was after five o'clock Friday. The courthouse closed at five. The sheriff's office was on the second floor with the tax collector's office, the register of deeds, the clerk of court and the county accountant.

Myrtle Godwin, the assistant clerk of court, was a pudgy woman who waddled and smiled like a mannequin. The clerk of court sold insurance in his private office and allowed Myrtle to run the office since she had authority equal to him.

Myrtle was the lead singer in the First Missionary Baptist Church in Hamlet. She developed a following of young girls between the ages of thirteen and eighteen. She was preparing them for marriage, she told the young women, with secrets that should be kept.

All of the young women she coached disappeared in college, married obscure men and adjusted to a life of anonymity.

Myrtle and her husband went their separate ways like two ships traveling randomly at sea. Myrtle pursued her public job and social duties and her husband dealt in pawnbroking jewelry.

A prisoner accidentally discovered she was having an affair with Sheriff Tate. She sometimes came to the sheriff's office between five and seven o'clock in the evening. If the sheriff wasn't busy, they would go to the jail, on the first floor beneath his office. A set of narrow steps led from the sheriff's office down to the room where he kept confiscated bootleg whiskey and guns. His dispatcher operated there and had access to the jail cells. The dispatcher did not come on duty until ten o'clock in the evening.

When the courthouse was built in 1939, the county attorney wanted to make a statement for justice and had the building designed so the bottom floor served as jail space for fifty prisoners, four times the need of a county with a population of nine thousand. There were always empty, isolated cells. It was in the empty cell section where the sheriff and Myrtle held their clandestine meetings.

He liked the way she kissed. Her lips were full and voluptuous. Her frog-like face was repugnant but the sheriff soon learned she longed to exhaust the passion which filled her. Her lips felt like an extension of her mouth, and her total sensuality fused with her mouth, tongue and lips. When she kissed the sheriff, it felt as if she had three tongues.

One night the constable, Chase Smith, put the town drunk, Robert Harrell, in the sheriff's recreational section by mistake. When the sheriff and Myrtle reached their spasmodic climax the sheriff kicked his shoes off and they fell on the floor and aroused Robert in the next cell. Robert listened through his drunkenness at the grunting and groaning from the adjoining cell. The sounds startled him. For a moment, he thought the sheriff was wrestling with a prisoner who was attempting escape. He rolled off his cot and staggered to the bars separating the cells.

"Sheriff!" he yelled, "is that you?"

The sheriff, taken by surprise, fell off the bunk.

"Are you hurt Sheriff?" Robert yelled again. "Did he hurt you? Let me at the sonofabitch."

Myrtle pulled her dress down and got off the bunk. Robert recognized her.

"I will be damn," he muttered, staggered and fell on his cot.

The sheriff grew up an honest man. His family were sharecroppers who taught him to work hard, do an honest days work, believe in God, hope for the best, and put his faith in the future. He chose to remain on the farm with his parents and care for them until they passed away.

Earl Tate collected fees for the service of court papers and a percentage of back taxes for his pay. His total yearly compensation was approximately three thousand dollars. The commissioners refused to increase his salary.

The sheriff and Myrtle were in close contact because Myrtle issued all papers from the court. They worked nights taking care of court business.

Myrtle suggested a way they could obtain money. The clerk of court received all court costs and fines and all monies collected by civil judgments. Myrtle used two receipt books. One for the defendant who paid the cost and fine, and the other for the auditor. Myrtle and Tate kept some of the money received through the defendant's book.

Tate at first refused to be a party to Myrtle's scheme, then decided he and his family had been stolen from for as long as he could remember. His parents related to him the years they ended up with nothing but the promise of another year to pay back a loss. He saw his mother and father go without dress clothes except church Sundays when his father wore clean khakis and his mother wore a homemade cotton dress. They were victims of an unending cycle of toil and sweat where all profits went to the landowner.

He had come to feel that justice was a role played outside his family. The only true justice was as the Bible said, "an eye for and eye, a tooth for a tooth."

The system had plucked his eye and his family's eye and heart. Now was his chance to pluck back.

His wife began sleeping in a separate bed. At first she said the smell of alcohol offended her. Finally she admitted to herself it was because he began to sleep in his clothes. He would go to his room, fall on his bed and sleep.

In the slow motion of his brain, the sheriff interpreted her action as kicking him out of bed. This did not change his habits because he felt she did not know his need to slow down, to let the disease run its course. The disease was the system, and he reasoned he was forced to be a part of it.

His affair with Myrtle became another way of stealing.

He was stealing honor and respect from himself, leaving emptiness he abhorred and tried to ignore. In his mind, the taking of money was taking back that taken from him and his family.

Whiskey, and sex with Myrtle, and the taking of money illegally, blended into a stealing from himself and society. Whiskey slowed things down and stole time from him and gave the disease time to run its course. Sex with Myrtle and taking the money sped things up, yet stopped time. Whiskey, sex and stealing took the blur out, suspended time, and his awareness, and this made time fly faster. He looked at time as a flashing light in a pit of darkness. Everything was stealing time.

After the district attorney left, the sheriff waited until six-thirty and Myrtle came through the door. He got up, put his black hat on and limped as he turned and started down the steps. Myrtle followed.

It was difficult for him to keep his suit clean because he sometimes slept in it. He used a whisk broom to keep the dust and lint off. His clothes crimped around his crotch and arm pits. His appearance was musty and slick.

Myrtle noticed the wrinkles around his armpits as she followed him downstairs.

Judge Alfice Moore

"Hold up a minute," Luke said as he stopped pushing, wiped his brow, gave a short gasp, and gazed at the house. He remembered Judge Moore lifting himself from the red leather chair, going to the window and gazing over the city of Raleigh.

Luke could smell the leather.

His nose was more sensitive after his headaches began. He smelled the rawhide and the fuming, tanning into the leather, and he smelled the heat spinning from the saw as it sped through the green walnut timber.

The judge's chamber reminded him of his study. Maroon leather chairs, an ottoman and a couch. Walnut panels from floor to ceiling. Book shelves, filled with the state laws and appellate decisions, history books and classic novels, covered the wall behind the judge.

"The outlawry proclamation is serious business, Luke," the judge said as he rolled a pencil unconsciously between his thumb and fingers. "Hasn't been one issued in North Carolina in I don't know how long. There were some issued during Reconstruction, I know."

Luke turned in his chair and watched Judge Moore's profile. Alfice Moore, a powerful man, stood six feet six inches tall and weighed two hundred fifty pounds. His body was hardened by lifting bushel baskets of apples on his father's farm. A short, blunted nose rose from his flat face like that of a prize fighter. Every summer from age sixteen to twenty-five he had worked in his father's orchard, saved his money and used it to attend undergraduate and law school.

Called by the nickname "Mountain Man" he was powerful physically, spiritually and intellectually. Judge Moore was top debater on his college team, and led the wrestling team to a conference title.

He took pleasure in knowing he had beaten out a liberal democrat for his judgeship.

A few years after he returned home, he was elected district attorney. After eight years, he was elected superior court judge. After twelve years on the bench, the conservative coalition recruited him to run for governor. The liberal candidate defeated him. He continued to sit as judge and was now thinking about running for the

United States Senate.

His experience as district attorney and judge taught him that the only time the law went strictly by the letter was in the appellate division. Even then decisions were based on social arguments instead of the letter of the law.

He engaged in many plea bargains and considered them a short circuit to justice. It was a necessary thing to speed the system, to cull it, that it may operate smoothly. Plea bargaining, in effect, was the bending of the law to make it go around the sharp curves society had to make at high speed.

"You say," Judge Moore continued as he rolled the pencil between his thumb and forefinger, gazing over the state capital of Raleigh as if he were asking it the question, "that this man carries a gun down the country road he lives on? Stops traffic and takes over his church and preaches naked, holding the congregation hostage?"

He turned to Luke as if the question was not enough, and his look, the confrontation, would outweigh the question.

Judge Moore did not want to issue the proclamation. It was like Pontius Pilate washing his hands, dispensing with Jesus.

"That's right. It's all on the petition here," Luke said as he laid the paper on the judge's desk.

"You realize, Luke, that this is the same as signing a death warrant on the man," Judge Moore said as he went to his desk and sat.

"I know it's serious, Judge, but our situation is serious. Very serious. He's got to be taken off the streets. If we allow this to go on unabated somebody is likely to get killed and the sheriff is done for in politics. He supports you and me, but this is not a political issue. This is an issue of what is right and what is wrong in our society. Just think, a naked man stopping the mail lady with a gun and turning her away from serving the United States mail."

"What does his congregation think about him taking over the church? Don't some of them want to do something about him?"

"They do. Some of them have been to us. They don't know what to do. They come to us to do something. Whatever is done, we'll have to do it."

"Has the man ever injured anyone? Has he ever shot or attempted to shoot anyone?"

The eyes of the judge and Luke drove at each other across the judge's desk and they began to feel the law bending, wavering.

"Our responsibility is to protect society." Luke flung the words toward Judge Moore like darts.

The judge blinked his eyes and said, "You're right. We must keep an ordered, safe society. It is our duty."

"Sometimes, Judge, we have to bend the law a little to do that." Luke looked blankly away from the judge at the bookcases behind the desk, and added, "We can't apply the same law to crazy people that we apply to ourselves. By that I mean a crazy person cannot follow man's civilized law."

"I'll agree with you on that. Everything is bent out of shape with the crazy person." Judge Moore again rolled the pencil with his fingers.

"Tell me about him," he added as he stood and walked to the window and gazed out. He felt the pressure of society bending the letter of the law as he knew it. Every sane person knows a crazy person cannot follow the letter of the law. An insane person is the most awful of all benders. He responds to absolutely no part of the law.

"He has intimidated people by walking naked down the road carrying his gun. I think it is the naked part that bothers the women more than anything else. It insults their dignity. It is humiliating and offensive to them. The white people are just not going to put up with it. This is not a white-black issue. The issue is whether the man is to continue doing this. It happens to be political because whites and Negroes are involved. But it shouldn't be. It's like a time bomb. We're just waiting for it to explode and we are the sitting ducks.

"There is a strange thing about colored people. The decent ones don't believe in suicide nor do they believe in killing someone else. There's not a single one in the congregation who would raise a weapon against him to bring him out of the church or take him to the courthouse. All refuse to take a warrant against him. But they come and plead for us to do something. You see what a mess we're in?"

The judge went behind his desk and sat, staring blankly at the bookshelves. After a few minutes he turned and faced Luke.

"The felony is the hostage deal with the congregation. Right?"

"Right." Luke replied.

"Okay, I'll sign it."

Luke Hampton

"It's malignant, Luke," the doctor said shortly before Luke talked to the sheriff about Wardell Burge.

Luke had been bothered with headaches for several months before his wife talked him into seeing his doctor.

"You don't have a history of headaches," Beverly told him, "and this means something organic could be wrong."

An appointment was scheduled with Dr. Parker, a member of the Presbyterian church which Luke and Beverly attended. He ordered a brain scan.

The scan showed a mass on the cerebellum. A biopsy was completed, and the doctor told Luke that the mass was malignant.

Beverly graciously attended all the social gatherings expected of the district attorney's wife. There was a gentle concern in her relationship with Luke. They had no children and most of their time was spent together. They attended each performance of the North Carolina Symphony in the area. Beverly and Luke lived in Morehead City and enjoyed area sail and speed boat races. They were pleased with their station in life.

Church was a social function to Luke. He attended because it was a custom for his family. It was observed from generation to generation that they attend church and believe in God, whom they believed available for them to call upon in time of need.

It was the Hampton family's tradition to make political and business contacts in the church system and make generous donations. This gave them what they thought to be special privileges with God and advantages in politics and business. It was beneficial politically for Luke to get membership listings from Presbyterian churches in his district and contact members personally or through correspondence.

With Luke, church had little to do with God on a personal level, or with death.

When Dr. Parker said, "it's malignant, Luke," going to church ceased to be a social tool for him. Suddenly the church became a harbor for God. Time suddenly became real. Things he did became real, took on different values.

Luke realized for the first time that life was real and death was a threat, lying in wait, hiding. The rumble of silence ran his pauses, destroying his time, his life.

Now he looked at himself as alone. The social functions of church, the camaraderie of his bar meetings, watching sail and speed boats mastering the water, all seemed unimportant and senseless.

As he continued to participate, he became profoundly and painfully aware that outside all the happenings, something more powerful and more permanent lurked beyond his consciousness. His life, to him, became inscrutable. He found he was fighting for life, but questioned what it was for. What was its value? Death was the enemy but where was it? He felt helpless. Luke had no armory to deflect the attack. He felt like a blind coward swinging wildly at an unthinkable adversary. The further he looked into the depth of being the deeper the doom. It was now, for him, an all-out battle of self-defense. He staked himself out on a lonely, desolate outpost, without weaponry, without hope.

Luke decided he was not going to give up the life he loved. He would continue his bourbon and medium rare steaks and his reading of the classics, the Bible and law books. He would continue his work as best he could.

Luke did not mention his cancer to anyone. He decided the burden was his alone.

"We will start radiation treatment Friday," Dr. Parker said.

Wardell Burge

Greg Butler pulled out his binoculars and scanned the house for Wardell Burge.

Al looked at the binoculars and then down the road as if he had gained the power to see through the walls of the house. He visualized Burge skulking inside.

The sheriff stopped, drew the bourbon from his pocket and took a drink.

"See anything, Greg?" he asked.

Greg continued to search the building slowly. "A little movement, it looks like, in the window on the top floor. But I can't tell what it is or who it is. That is, if it is a person."

The sheriff limped behind him and said, "We got to

be careful. His mama is living in there with him. We sure don't want nothing to happen to her. And him neither if we can help it. We want him to come out if he will. We don't want to shoot him unless we have to."

Al Jackson's teeth grated and he kept pounding the house with his eyes. This is one time I'm going to do my thing, he thought. "See anything yet?" he asked softly, as if hiding the words from Burge.

"Yeah. I saw a man pass the window. I take it to be Burge."

"Here, let me have the glasses." The sheriff, wobbling, took the binoculars and looked at the house.

Greg smelled the whiskey on the sheriff's breath and squinted.

"Yeah. He's in there," the sheriff grunted, "that's Wardell."

Wardell Burge was born January 16, 1923 in Ownes County, on the Catfish Lake Road where he now resides. His family owned a small farm and sustained themselves with the produce of hogs, cows, corn, tobacco, cabbage, collards, beans and squash.

Wardell had two brothers and a sister. They graduated from high school and attended college in Waterbury, Connecticut. The sister became a teacher. One brother went into law and the other into medicine. They seldom returned.

When Wardell grew up, the Catfish Lake Road was unpaved. Catfish Lake, at the end of the road, was five miles across, and lay six miles in the midst of a dense pocosin forest. The pocosin was a federal reserve area regulated by the Federal Wildlife Commission.

Wardell was the youngest of the children and he was at home without siblings from age twelve. Sometimes he would walk the dirt road toward Catfish Lake thinking about his brothers and sister. His father died when Wardell was ten and he had only his mother and grandmother at home.

During those long walks he would occasionally believe that in reality he would find his brothers and his sister in the forest. At times he would sit by the roadside and imagine he could see them coming down the road or out of the woods. There were times he saw bear and panther crossing the road but he was not afraid. He would turn their images into his brothers and sister.

The deep, dark, mysterious forest and its humming wildlife became a secret part of him. He did not hunt it. He shared it. It twirled and twisted in his imagination and became his hidden family.

In 1943, Wardell was drafted into the Army. His nation was at war, and it was the duty of every male between the ages of eighteen and thirty-five to serve in the armed forces and protect democracy. He became a shuddering, fearful bundle of nerves, but he generated enough courage to follow instructions. If he had to, he would fight for his country.

Wardell went through basic training and was placed

in the quartermaster division. He drove trucks carrying supplies to the front line in Italy. He carried supplies to soldiers during the siege of Casino. The momentum shifted back and forth as the Americans took Casino and the Germans recaptured it. He saw the city change hands three times.

His buddy was critically wounded by an artillery shell that blew up his truck. He was able to overcome his fear and he generated enough courage to rush without thinking through the exploding fire to the truck and throw his coat over the screaming soldier and snuff the flames. His comrade suffered third-degree burns.

Wardell received the Purple Heart and a Bronze Star. Although he attained the rank of sergeant, he accepted his discharge immediately after the war.

Wardell did not like the Army, nor the war. He liked the killing even less.

Comparing his military service to his life in North Carolina, Wardell felt a deepening chasm between himself and white people. He had felt that way from early childhood because he went to different schools, churches and theaters, and used different bathrooms, water fountains, and bus seats than white people.

At first it seemed the whites and blacks were cut into different pieces and put in different blocks like checkers on a checker board where they checked and slew each other. They weren't whole people but bits and pieces of people who were separated so the whole person wouldn't know who they were. It was like being dead and alive simultaneously.

Then it seemed like black and white alike were chopped up and separated and made unknown to themselves and each other.

The military was the same. They slept in different houses and went to different movies. It was like an invisible wall nobody could tear down or go over, existed between white and black individuals.

He thought white people were persecuting him because he felt they were the ones who built the wall. He faulted his mother and all other blacks because they let the whites do it. As far as he was concerned everybody was persecuting him. He kept that secret. It was something he thought nobody would understand and he didn't think they wanted to. There was something about his secret that he feared but he didn't know what it was.

When Wardell returned from the war, he began again to take long walks down the newly-paved Catfish Lake Road. According to local democrats, Governor Scott Privette paved every country road that had an outhouse.

The hardtop highway ended at the Burge home and the dirt road continued to Catfish Lake. The lake was once a huge juniper forest. Fire ravaged the forest and the trees died, creating a basin which formed the lake. Wardell walked the dirt road continuously. Sometimes he would walk to the lake on a path hacked by intrepid hunters. He would sit on a fallen juniper and watch alligators take turtles from the surface, and he watched hawks, like missiles, burst feathers from ducks. In the shallows near him, he watched bass taking bream and raccoon eating mussels and tiny turtles. Once he saw a small bear dismembered as it swam into the lake.

During those times he began to imagine that the animals were turning into people. They were only forms but he felt they were people. Little people and big people, wrestling and playing with each other, and eating each other. Fighting and driving away each other.

He did not like that. It frightened him and he decided he would not go to the lake anymore.

One night as he lay in bed, he smelled and tasted the dark. He often had trouble sleeping because the images he saw of animals at the lake would return. Sometimes they would become his brothers and sister and his mother and grandmother. Other times they would be the war and noise and blood mixed into the water of the lake and the blackness of his mind. The dark smelled and tasted like fine metal filings of copper, zinc, brass, lead, iron, gold and silver, all milled into dust and mixed with his blood. He could smell it, taste it, hear it racing through his body, echoing in his mind.

To him, darkness became denigration.

Eventually he lay in bed experiencing the ultimate of smelling and hearing and tasting the darkness of his blood, and he saw the whites of his eyes out in space with nothing in them. For the first time, he could smell his skin and the bed where he had lain his unwashed body for the past six months.

It was then he decided he had to preach.

The sounds of motion, the grinding of the minerals, the roiling of his blood, and the rattling of his darkness became voices. The animals of the forest began talking.

He heard Jesus talking in a puny voice. Small compared to the rush of other voices, and the plants blooming and grabbing from earth to sky shouting in soft motion. He could hear them all.

Everything became mere forms, shadows, and voices. His feelings became huddled masses of fear harboring in his soul. He felt his fears were being frightened out of him.

He felt himself fearfully in the midst of all things, yet nowhere.

Burge got up softly in his dark, naked, walked down the black asphalt road to the church, felt his way to the pulpit and preached into the compassionless dark.

Before he started talking, all the metal he tasted flowing and tumbling through his blood turned into millions of tiny bells, chiming and clanging. In one great harmonizing swoop they consumed him into words.

"I am come naked to shame and to be shamed and to tell that the blood is the problem. It's a problem with the blood. Oh perfect blood! I plead and bled for perfect blood but it never come. I fought everything out there and I cried up in the sky and let my tears run down the mountainside and make ponds, like eyes in the earth, and I argued with the devil who came from way yonder back inside me and out of everybody else. The blood is the problem, it's a problem with the blood, it's a problem with the blood. Oh perfect blood! I plead and bled for perfect blood."

For two weeks in a row Wardell rose in the middle of the night and marched under the starry sky to the church and preached. Most of the time he preached the same sermon, then slipped back to his room and slept.

On Sunday morning, April 12, 1965, Wardell, naked, left his house carrying a twenty-two caliber rifle. He went to his church. When he entered, the congregation groaned, in a prolonged expiration, and hushed. Their eyes followed him in shame and shock as he walked down the center aisle to the pulpit carrying the gun over his shoulder, like he had done as a soldier in Italy.

The preacher, a small wizened man with horn-rimmed glasses, was shocked. He turned when Wardell ascended the steps and faced him. He drew enough courage to yell, "Wardell! You get out of here, boy, and get some clothes on!"

Wardell took the gun from his shoulder and motioned the preacher to sit. Then he turned to the pulpit and laid the gun across it. The barrel pointed over the heads of the congregation. The only sounds were the slipping of shoe soles on the floor.

Wardell Burge had powerful muscles, curving long and full, roping his bone structure. His color was bronze. His face contorted. Behind the contortion there was a strained calmness in his eyes that attempted to restrain the terror in him.

He stood behind the pulpit dripping with sweat. His face and lips were wet. His forearms glistened as if greased with oil as he reached the Bible with faltering fingers. He turned the pages at random, then suddenly stopped and looked at the congregation.

The members moved and acted as if welded together by the appearance and actions of Burge. Eyes covered his body. Hearts fluttered when he touched the gun. Ears waited fearfully for his lips to move. They felt the anguish on his face. They began to sweat as Burge's body gleamed. When his fingers turned the pages of the Bible, it was as if he were unlocking doors secret and private in their beings. They were terrified; yet juxtaposed against that terror was a depth of compassion they could not understand.

"I am come naked to shame and be shamed, when I heard the voice and then the voices. The Meek Man cometh unto me and I cast him out! Then the Big Man cometh and I let him stay," he began.

The congregation stirred and the preacher twisted in his seat. Burge touched the gun and hush resumed.

"God walked into me!" His voice rumbled through the church in a deep baritone. "I was lying flat my back and

God walked upright into me. He walked into my body and I shattered and come apart and there was nothing left in me but my eyes and all I was doing was seeing. Because my blood rushed out, too, and I knew the trouble was in the blood, it's a problem with the blood. The blood is in the sin and the sin is in the blood because the blood passes the sin along and the sin passes the blood along. I tell because the voice is in me, has come to me and turned into many voices, because out of the one voice comes many voices and I have become a voice."

Sweat dripped off his elbows, his chin, ran from his forehead into his eyes, and from his armpits down his stomach to his groin. Tears poured from his eyes and flowed and mixed with the sweat.

The congregation stirred and the preacher opened his mouth to speak.

Burge touched the gun.

"I have plead and bled for perfect blood. I have carried my blood to the mountaintop and mixed it with my tears and poured them down the mountain, freed my tears and blood to let them wash the peaks, the slopes, and fill the valleys where they stand and shimmer like hungry eyes.

"When I became nothing but eyes I saw all the animals, every kind and description, even more than was on the ark, rushing out of me like they had been run out of a terrible forest into a peaceable clearing where they all ate the same food, and bats, fowl of the air, came out screaming and all the vicious things that I thought was not me came out, rushed out, into a freedom, and all the plants rushed out of me blooming and the flowers and the trees rushed out of me in a giant whirlwind and pitched in the clearing, the free place, and I was left naked with nothing but my skin and vision beholding."

Sweat mixed with tears ran like little rivulets down his body into a puddle on the varnished oak floor.

The preacher's shirt stuck to his skin, his coat was sullied, and his face fixed in awe. Several members moved to rise. Burge touched his gun.

Hush came again.

"I am the vision and the voice, come to see and say it all."

Wardell preached until two in the afternoon. There was nothing left in him but the ravages of his words and exhaustion. His body, his spirit, felt as if a mysterious force had devoured them and suddenly leapt from his being.

He picked up his gun, placed it on his shoulder, walked down the aisle and out the church, into the sun, then down the black, slick asphalt road to his home.

Burge's House

"Let's hold up here a minute and see what he does," the sheriff said as he limped slowly in a semicircle, holding the house with his eyes.

They stopped. Al adjusted his gun belt and smiled as he fingered the twelve-gauge shells. "You just as well come out, 'cause we're gonna git your ass, Burge," he said with spurs on his words.

"Shut up," the sheriff said and again limped slowly in a semicircle, holding the house with his eyes.

His limp was the result of a mule kick when he was nine. He was flat-breaking ground, and in making a turn a trace came loose from the plow. While he was attempting to re-hook the trace the mule kicked him viciously on the side of his knee. The wound pained him but he managed to get by without going to a doctor. He favored the wound with a limp which he was never able to discard.

He unconsciously developed his limp into a soft rhythmic flow. His injured leg rose and descended softly as if the motion itself were protecting the ancient injury, giving his movements a dreamlike quality.

The sheriff knew the wound failed to heal and he wanted everyone else to know it.

His head sat askew as the result of another childhood accident. He fell from a wagon, landed on his head, and severely strained his neck. He was not taken to a doctor. Pain caused his head to lean considerably to the left.

Luke and Greg gave Al a puzzled look, then shifted their eyes to the house.

"I hope we can get him without any trouble," Luke said passively.

"Me too," Greg said, adding, "but we are going to have to get him one way or the other."

"Yes," Luke agreed.

"That's right," the sheriff added.

Greg wiped his lips. "Got a Coke or something in the boot, Sheriff?" he asked.

"Al, did you put them Cokes that was in the cooler in the boot?" the sheriff asked.

"Yeah," Al answered and quickly unlocked the trunk of the car. "Who wants one?" he inquired.

"I'll take one," Greg responded.

"Believe I will too," said Luke.

Al took one for himself. The sheriff looked at them and smiled.

"Well, hell, if ya'll are gonna drink one I am too." He laughed.

The wind lulled. The four men were still, except for tipping their Cokes, and for a moment they watched the house. Pine, gum and oak trees stood stark like figurines, as if frozen for a lifeless moment, suspended motionless in time.

The house glowed in the distance as if internal energy were beginning the slow, inexorable, irrefutable secret of motion and its unknown results.

A dark cloud hung overhead. Crows called from the stillness of the forest.

"Think it's going into a steady rain, Sheriff?" Luke asked.

"Donno," the sheriff replied as he crooked his head toward the cloud. "Hope it don't but it shore looks like it will."

"Wonder what's wrong with the man?" Greg asked as he tipped his Coke.

The sheriff, Greg, and Luke looked at the house and pondered the question as if trying to extract the answer with the force of sheer will, and solve the problem on the spot.

"I don't care what's wrong with him," Al said as he

adjusted his cap. "That ain't for us to figure out. That's his problem." He drank his Coke and licked his lips.

"Didn't you say he didn't act right when he came home from the war, Sheriff?" Luke asked.

"Yeah." The sheriff swallowed a sip of Coke and moved his eyes from Luke to the house. "They say he made a big change when he come home. He didn't act right. They said he used to go to the lake a lot before he went off but since he come home he don't never hardly ever go there anymore."

He continued to look at the house and took another sip of Coke. "Okay," the sheriff said as he handed the binoculars to Greg, "let's get a little closer."

The three men began pushing the car again.

The sun, flickering between showers, the black asphalt road glistening like a dormant snake, the men pushing the cruiser, combined as if all had grown into one. The sheriff, limping behind them as if recently wounded, the gum, pine and oak trees alongside the road stirring restlessly in the wind, and the home of Wardell Burge looming in the curve as if it were about to take wings and transcend time, space and events, all mixed and created an ethereal quality.

It was as if none of it belonged in the world of reality, as if it were in a world of its own, created from its own energy and at any moment it would suddenly evaporate, vanish into the source of dreams and leave no trace of ever existing.

"See anything?" the sheriff asked, pushing his hat up and wiping his brow.

Al Jackson stood straight, adjusted his gun belt and peered beneath the rim of his cap toward the house. He began thinking about tonight. He would wrestle with Amy. Wednesday night was set aside for their wrestling. That was the night his wife played bridge. If there was no emergency for the department, then Wednesday was their night.

They called sex wrestling because Al like to serve Amy from the top, holding her wrists riveted to the bed. He made her use pillows to make her more vulnerable to his thrust and he felt he could give her his full measure. That was not enough. There was always something left, unfinished, after he had exhausted himself with all his force and power emptying into her. All the pounding, all the grasping and all her sighing of completeness seemed to leave him vacuous, like a spent shell.

She seemed completely satisfied to him, a fragment of life, fulfilled briefly like a firefly blinks on and off before death. He thought of her as a nest of fireflies blinking on and off.

Flickers of satisfaction passed through him, but emptiness followed and roosted like a vulture on a broken tree limb.

The juxtaposition of pleasure against the emptiness that followed was a mystery to Al. He chose to harbor the fleeting moments of satisfaction he experienced when Amy sighed and broke open in ecstasy upon climax.

Following years barren of sex, Amy felt a secret victory, a monumental fulfillment, as the man of power, the law enforcer, dismounted and lay briefly on the bed, breathing heavily into the emptiness of time. She knew she did not have all she wanted but she had learned that having sex was better than having nothing at all. It obliterated the lonely hours she spent at home, during which she would take forest walks to see how many plants and trees she could identify and how many bird voices she could imitate.

She wanted someone to live with her and let her love him, because to her it was easier to give herself to someone else than try to figure herself out. She did not like to think about herself. Al was more a part of her than she was.

"Robert's been acting up again," she said one night after Al dismounted and lay smoking a Camel.

"What's he doing now?"

"You know how crazy he is. Taking them tranquilizers and things so long he can't think straight. He's giving me part of his disability check. And he called the other day and said he was thinking about stopping it. He's heard about you coming here. He suspects something but don't nobody know nothing about what's going on except me and you. You ain't said nothing to nobody, have you?"

Al blew a grey cloud toward the ceiling and relaxed. "Hell no. Robert's the one that's crazy. You don't think I'm crazy too, do you?"

"I know you ain't. But your car is being parked here right much. Thought people had asked you about it. You know the way people talk."

"When they ask me I tell 'em what's his name called and threatened and I am making prevention calls. There ought to be a call like that. Yeah! I'll suggest that to the sheriff. We'll put prevention calls on our schedule. Ain't you got your separation papers?"

"Yeah."

"Well, soon as you get your divorce I'm going to separate and get my divorce and then we'll get married. Frances thinks something is going on with me but she don't have no idea what. She knows I have to make all these calls on domestic violence. She knows better'n talk crazy stuff on me. I'll just tell her to get her ass out. I'm the law. I've always treated her all right but we really ain't never been all in gear together. But when we get together she takes control. Like back in her mind she does it for a service. She has a lot of bad headaches and don't feel like it much. Specially since I have been coming here. She might smell it. Sometimes people smell things like that. But it don't make no difference. We'll take care of things when they come up."

He grabbed for her pelvis and rubbed, as his mouth turned into a joker's smile.

Murray Whittier

"Saw a little movement on the curtain on the bottom floor. Can't make out who it is," Greg announced.

A small grey cloud sped at an angle from the house toward the men. Rain fell in silver sheets, shunting with the wind currents, bringing with it the sound of thousands of raindrops rushing upon the earth like padded hooves.

The men shielded their faces with their forearms. The cloud passed quickly in a rushing, twirling, silver downpour of sound, crossed the road, and disappeared into the green entangled forest.

"Here. Let me look." Luke said. He took the binoculars and scanned long and steady, examining every crevice in the building. Like a dog waiting for his master's command, Al watched Luke.

"I saw something move, I believe it was a curtain. It might be the wind," Luke said, handing the binoculars to Greg.

"We want to be sure. It's Burge we're after. We want to be doubly sure nobody's in there but Burge. We don't want to hurt him unless we have to," the sheriff said as he mopped his face.

The sheriff had never killed anything with a gun, nor whipped the mules when he was a sharecropper. He talked to them like he talked to people under arrest, "come along now, come along now," he would say softly as he pulled easily at the lines on the mule or the arm of a prisoner. Usually the mule responded the second time he called, and the prisoner when the sheriff added, "I'll talk to the judge and keep you out of jail."

When Tate left the Hammond plantation as a sharecropper, he swore if he ever got an honorable job he would wear a three-piece suit.

When he became sheriff, he left the pistol he used as deputy in his desk drawer and went to a full three-piece suit, and a black Stetson.

Today he wore a small red feather tucked in his hatband. A piece of adhesive tape was across his left eyebrow. Luke asked him that morning what happened and he answered, "walked into a door," and chuckled, "that's what they all say ain't it?"

He had fallen from a jail cot where he sometimes slept off his weariness.

The sheriff and Murray Whittier, the clerk of superior court, were political cronies.

Whittier was a tall, freckled, bald man. The freckles moved up his face and across the top of his head. His emotionless blue eyes glittered, keeping the same lidless immobility whether he was laughing or in deep concentration. The latter he did very seldom because Murray was limited in mental dexterity. He had rather chuckle than try to figure things out.

He came to work every day in suit and tie and in his private office sold insurance and held meetings for the Democratic Party.

The last of a long line of aristocratic Whittiers, Murray was a proud man. He lived with his two sisters in the old homeplace.

His marriage to Anita Barfield in the early forties lasted only a week. Anita was a suffragette. She was active in the Democratic Party. Murray, being involved in state-level politics and being the custodian over his family's affairs, was considered a good catch. Their courtship was cordial and formal, like peacocks displaying plumes. They never kissed until their wedding night.

Anita was a passionate woman who was humiliated when denied the pleasures which she considered a luxury of matrimony. On her wedding night she found Murray incapable of performing the services she sought.

She promptly returned to Kinston and openly proclaimed, for what she called her own honor, his lack of bedroom prowess. The talk was hushed in Ownes County and Murray continued to drive his two sisters to church and shopping with pompous ease.

His father, wanting to ensure a cultured background for him, sent him to boarding school. He returned home qualified to teach elementary grades in the public school system. He was better at throwing erasers at students than teaching. He relegated himself to substitute teacher and took over management of the plantation.

Tending the farm, Murray insisting on plowing with coat, tie, straw hat, and patent leather shoes. He soon learned that it was an expensive venture to keep new shoes and to keep his clothes properly laundered.

The mule, one of the most stubborn of all nature's creatures, caught Murray unaware. Unknowing to Murray the mule resented being on hand to pull a plow, wagon or log, or to be at the mercy of screeching children who wished to ride on Sundays. The mule developed its own means of retaliation and revenge. For its keep, it would remain in bondage as beast of burden, for which it would exchange kicks and expel flatulence at will. Kicking was reserved for times the mule was being thrashed with plow lines. Flatulence was reserved for plowing in the sultry, humid heat of May and June.

The beast, as Murray called it, had learned to curl its tail up and over, like the whirl of a question mark, allowing full expulsion of gas.

Rhythmic pooping of pootings insulted and infuriated Murray. He would thrash and curse, using expletives he never uttered in public, but the rhythmic flatulence would continue. What infuriated Murray most was that the flatulence expelled in rhythm with the mule's step. This was a cold calculation by the mule, Murray decided.

Farming became too closely related to work for Murray and he retired from what he called, "the whole mess of it." He more than welcomed words of Hammond, chairman to the Board of Commissioners, "Murray, the clerk of court's office is going to be vacant soon. We are going to hafta' remove Collins for malfeasance. You know he stays drunk all the time. How would you like to have it?"

He didn't mind, later, when Hammond told him he should hire a homely girl to work as his assistant. "To keep the gadflies out of your office. Tate knows a good many of that sort. Talk to him about it."

Myrtle had taken a two-year bookkeeping course and soon earned the trust of Murray and his close friends. Sheriff Tate had known her since he was deputy. He bought trinkets and Christmas cards from her at her husband's shop. She and the sheriff were subtly attracted. They did not declare their feelings or motives, but did their thing, as they called it.

She got sex education by watching her brothers masturbate behind the barn. This aroused sexual energy in her which she abhorred. It seemed they were voraciously stealing from themselves and spilling wastage upon the land. To her it was a horrific display of self-destruction. She further enhanced her education by watching the bull and jackass display their sexual organs and put them to work. She had a perfect view from her bedroom window to the barn and pasture where the animals were kept. In her view, the female of the species was brutalized at every sexual encounter. So she sought the soft solace of young women and liked it.

Myrtle's sexual preference was not for the males and she faked orgasm in her encounters with the sheriff. There was some pleasure for her but it didn't compare with that shared with her women. She called that pleasure and feeling, pure pleasure, pure feeling.

She was a private and secretive person who went back and forth quietly and did her duties as if under secret orders. No one paid any attention when she began driving new cars. Only the county commissioners knew the salary and they believed her husband, Selby Godwin, was earning sufficient income in his jewelry, clock, watch and pawnbroking shop to provide these luxuries.

When she began buying cars for her special girls, however, the public began to question where the money was coming from.

Anna Noble

Wardell Burge peered through the curtain crack.

The animals are coming. Ganged together, grinding out sounds. In a ball, their legs are moving from their white body. Coming from one body churning slowly. Strange animals with red skin and dark hair. Carrying sticks and making strange sounds. A gorilla. A tiger. A bear. Alligator. Coming toward me trying to get back inside me. Trying to tear back inside me to fill me back up with themselves. They are going to eat my flesh and go into my blood and take control of my blood and my mind and I will be them and they will be me.

He turned, stirred the corn shucks with his feet and touched the rusty corn sheller. This is where he sometimes shelled corn. He turned and looked out the back window. There was no curtain. He had a clear view of the hog pen a short distance from the yard. A sow and three pigs ate soaked corn from a trough beneath an oak tree. A mocking bird sang from a pine bough.

Burge looked at the sow and three pigs and they became raging demons.

His mother left by the back door carrying a bucket of slops in one hand. She supported herself with a walking cane with her other hand. He watched her pick her way through the dog fennel to the hog pen and empty the slops into the trough across the fence. The hogs attacked the slops with noisy gulps.

Wardell feared for his mother's life. Feared the animals would eat her too. His eyes narrowed until the whites glared. Sweat began to cover his naked body. He turned from the window and lay down in the corn shucks. He began to cry and the shucks crackled and made crying sounds to him.

They are crying because they are shucks. They are used and no good and they are crying because they are empty and crying is all there is left for them to do. There is nothing else.

Yesterday Burge held up the mail carrier. He stopped her from passing down the Catfish Lake Road. His body glistened like a seal as he stood holding the gun barrel toward the ground. Anna Noble flushed with insult. Burge said not a word. He stood and looked down the middle of the road, as if he were a statue. His eyes twisted with internal madness. Anna's eyes drove wildly at him. Her body began to shake. She jerked the car into reverse and backed speedily to N.C. Highway 58.

Burge had done the same thing before and Anna raged her complaint to the sheriff.

"Sheriff, if you knew how I felt!" She explained, "not only did it scare me to death but I have never been so mortified. It was such an outrageous display of indecency. Do something with that man!"

She paused, regained her composure, and continued, "when it gets so the United States mail can be stopped by one man then something is bad wrong with our law."

"We'll do something, Anna. I promise you that," the sheriff said.

Wardell's mother cautiously returned down the path, through the overgrown weeds between the yard and hog pen, to the house with her empty slop bucket.

Burge peeped through the small crack in the curtain.

The animals have stopped. Their voices are crashing against each other. They are angry, cruel and murderous. Plotting to get me. They will come and eat the building and then eat me.

"Let's stop here a minute and see what he's doing," the sheriff said. "See if we can get a handle on him. What he's up to." The sheriff lit a cigarette.

"Good idea," Luke said, then added, "Don't strike until the iron is hot."

"What'cha mean by that?" Al asked.

"Get everything right," the sheriff said.

Greg Butler sheathed the binoculars and stared at the house. Maybe this would be the time he could strike one clear crack of the rifle for justice. He knew there had to be justice of some kind. It was best swift and certain. Yet there was a gnawing feeling inside him, trying to tell him he didn't really like his job. He thought about little Greg. What impression would he make on him? If he killed Wardell Burge, would that be a secret to himself?

He quickly put his disquietude aside and looked again toward the house as the car began to crawl forward.

Angra Kain

Angra Kain was an ambitious Hamlet attorney who was the first in his family to attain the status of a professional. In 1960 he began his quest for power in Ownes County.

Angra was born on a plantation named Hornets Nest in the northwest part of the county. The lush farmland, obtained by his great-grandfather, Nash Kain, prior to the Civil War, was located at the confluence of Tuskeet Creek and Flint River. By collaborating with the Yankees during the War and Reconstruction the family held on to their land. Three Kain men deserted the Confederate Army and joined with Yankee forces at New Berne in 1864. Captured by the Confederates, they were tried and hanged at Kinston the next year.

After the Civil War, the Kain family, strong closet republicans, gained possession of the postmaster's position in Hamlet and kept it well into the twentieth century. John Kain, Angra's father, moved to Hamlet with his wife and two sons when Angra was five.

Angra was six foot three inches tall, and star center on the Hamlet basketball team which won the state championship in 1932. He was the most valuable player in the tournament and easily won a college basketball scholarship.

During childhood he had a strange method of expressing displeasure. When participating in sports, if things did not go his way he would lie down on his stomach, beat his hands and fists on the ground or floor, and scream to the top of his voice. Angra carried this habit with him throughout high school and college.

He graduated from college and upon recommendation of his congressman entered the Navy as an ensign and remained for the duration of the Second World War. After the war he tried coaching and teaching, which became meaningless to him. He found little pay and no substantive power in either.

John Kain advised Angra to join the Democratic Party because in Ownes County you had to be a democrat to gain power in government. He told his son that since the Civil War, Ownes County voter registration was 98 percent democrat. The county was devastated during the

War by depredations inflicted on the populace by Yankees quartered at New Berne and Rebel forces at Kinston. Reconstruction brought even greater strife and turmoil to the area, he would say.

The pathway to power was through the legal profession where there was much money to be earned, according to the elder Kain.

John Kain, the postmaster, knew the president of Wake Forest University and their friendship secured his son admission to the School of Law. Angra graduated, passed the bar, came back to Hamlet and went into practice with Don Davis. Davis, a powerful state senator, ran for governor in 1960. As his campaign treasurer, Angra used campaign funds to buy the Negro vote in Ownes County and elect hand-picked boards of commission and education that year.

Sworn in on the first Monday in January, 1961, both boards immediately fired their attorney, Hugh Stanley, and hired Angra.

Two years later the sheriff and clerk of court ran unopposed. Angra knew that the sheriff and the clerk were friends and could control the Negro vote for their respective offices. Murray Whittier refused to join forces with Angra, because the recently fired county attorney and Whittier were political allies.

Whittier recommended clients to Stanley, the former county attorney. Unknown to Whittier, Angra sent his clients into the clerk's office to ask Whittier to suggest a good lawyer. Whittier would invariably recommend Stanley.

It was Angra's goal to remove Whittier from the clerk's office. He believed Whittier was an unwitting pawn, put in office by those who wished to use him. The clerk perceived himself a symbol of respect and capable for the office he held. Yet he was no match, in guile and political instinct, for Angra Kain.

Angra learned the requirements of the auditing procedures for the county offices. He knew audits should be available for public inspection. He could not find a single audit report for the clerk's or sheriff's office.

"We're going to have to do something about the lack of audits in the clerk's and sheriff's office, Harold."

Angra sprawled in his chair with one leg across the corner of his desk. He inserted his forefinger in his right nostril, worked it gently, and removed it. He was talking to the newly-elected chairman of the Board of Commissioners, Harold Sands.

A wealthy farmer, Sands had been close to Angra's family for years. Angra had no trouble convincing him to run for the board. Both men believed in conservative spending and thought that every public office should account for the monies at their disposal. That is the way Harold ran his farm. Harold looked to Angra when making major decisions on the board and depended entirely on him when legal matters arose.

"What can we do about it?" Harold asked.

"The county commissioners have the power to order audits if they have not been performed according to law. I suggest the commissioners order audits of the clerk's office."

"Okay, I'll have Horace to make the motion."

Angra took his leg off the corner of his desk, sat upright and pulled a fifth of Old Taylor, his favorite brand of bourbon, out of his desk drawer.

Murray's Audit

The first Monday of April 1965 the Board of Commissioners ordered audits to begin immediately on the clerk's office.

The auditor who served the county was an elderly man, Ray Jenkins, who annually audited the tax office and prepared budget proposals for the county. He was a political ally of Murray Whittier. They played bridge together, attended the area cocktail parties and were active in Democratic Party activities. Murray referred to Ray as his dear friend.

After the first day of the audit, Jenkins told Murray that it was urgent they talk.

"How urgent?" Murray asked.

"Tonight."

They met in Murray's private office.

"I'm finding some damaging irregularities, Murray. That's the only way I know to put it." Ray told him.

Murray's cold, lidless eyes stared from an emotionless face.

"Irregularities? What do you mean, Ray?" The words implied shock but the expression on Murray's face revealed nothing. Laughing nervously, he lit a cigarette. His bald head reflected a dull glow.

"I know there is nothing wrong with the way this office is run."

"So far, the judgment dockets and the entries in the minute docket, which show costs and fines, far outdistance the receipt ledger," Jenkins said.

Murray continued to stare candidly at him. He knew nothing of judgment dockets nor the minutes taken during court proceedings. He had never read one through. The clerk knew only how to swear a witness in court, to empanel the jury, and take oaths for probate. For political purposes, Murray was visible to the voters. He had not looked over Myrtle's shoulder a single time while she was filling out ledgers for the system. She insisted on doing the bookkeeping after hours, either on weeknights or weekends.

"In fact, sixty thousand dollars. And I'm just half through the audit." Ray's eyes were driving at Murray with an intensity that transcended friendship.

Murray thumped his cigarette several times, watching the ashes scatter like gunpowder in the tray. He stared into the tray with a look of inquisitive incomprehension, thinking about his situation with remote indifference. Like a goat looks at a dog just before the dog goes for its throat.

"Hadn't somebody made a mistake?" Murray asked. He moved the cigarette to his mouth as the smoke curled around his nose and eyes.

"I haven't. Maybe Myrtle?" Ray said.

"You think she fully understands bookkeeping?"

"I don't know but when I finish she'll have to do some explaining to somebody."

"How long do you think it'll take to finish?"

"At the rate I'm going, considering the mess it's in, the remainder of the week."

That was Monday night.

On Tuesday morning before the courthouse opened, Myrtle sat in the sheriff's office.

"I'm afraid they've caught us." Myrtle said. Murray had called her after Ray talked to him. Her thin lips swelled and rolled out voluptuously with perfect round sounds. Her eyes lay firmly on the sheriff and her face was fixed with a strange, secret pleasure.

She looked upon the sheriff as a source of protection. She gave him the small twist of pleasure he desired and in return they conspired to embezzle county funds.

"What are you talking about?" the sheriff asked. He

looked down and thumped his ashes.

"The auditors. Yesterday they came and by the day's end they found a lot of money missing."

"They did?"

"I didn't know they'd go through the minute dockets."

Sheriff Tate took a deep drag off his cigarette and blew it with his mouth fully open with a grey-blue blast toward the ceiling.

"Tell you what," he said looking through the smoke. "Accidentally leave all the books and money in the front office tonight when the auditor leaves and you close. Don't take nothing to the vault."

As custodian of the building, the sheriff had keys to every office in the courthouse. The clerk's front office had two windows and one door. The sheriff had a key to the door leading to the hall running the center of the second floor. That Tuesday night the clerk of court's office was allegedly broken into and an amount of cash, and many records disappeared. Someone entered the office through an outside window. Estimated cash missing was four thousand dollars. Also taken were criminal and civil cost sheets which reflected costs and fines for several years.

"Had them out there for the auditor," Myrtle said as casually as if she were serving coffee and donuts at a social function. "He probably forgot to put them back in the vault."

Myrtle spent the following two weeks in the hospital. She had been going to the doctor for the past year because of excessive tiredness and minor but constant weight loss. After a series of tests, the doctors detected an imbalance of red and white corpuscles and malformed platelets. Frequent blood transfusions held the disease in abeyance. The imbalance of red and white corpuscles continued and the malformed platelets slowly increased.

Angra conferred with Ray about the audit and considered his next move. There was evidence embezzlement had occurred but the break-in was causing complications. The records and the money being audited were missing. Nothing was left except the incomplete audit. Angra believed Murray did not have sense enough to embezzle. Myrtle was the culprit but Murray was responsible. A court conviction would be unlikely. There was no way to get figures from missing records.

The district attorney reluctantly accepted the explanation, fully understanding the burden of managing the office fell exclusively on the clerk. Luke worked with the clerk and sheriff, therefore did not want to bring charges.

Angra began speaking as he slid down in his chair and propped his right jaw in his hand, "Luke, you've seen the audit report as best the auditor could show. It's obvious the bookkeeping was very irregular. Enough so we should suspect embezzlement."

Angra paused, coiled his body and inserted his forefinger in his right nostril. "I don't want charges brought against Murray but you know something's got to be done. We can't let this thing go without doing something." He clasped his hands across his stomach and stared at Luke.

Luke knew Angra was right. He also knew the charges would be very difficult to prove. It would tear the county apart because Murray was highly respected and Angra's followers, chiefly outspoken rednecks, were a vociferous bunch.

They looked at each other, pondering a legal resolution. Angra, in the long run, seeking the downfall of Murray. Luke wanting to salvage respect for Murray and prevent his indictment.

Luke's flesh hung slack on his face. Small hollows formed just below his cheek bones. He was beginning to lose hair from the radium treatments.

More than a simple audit concerned him; more than an indictment against Murray. He was concerned, yes, but the deeper concern was the summons he knew that had been issued for his life and the demand was urgent, the results merciless, swift, and inevitable. This was his secret. Death was the inevitable seal each person carried, inexorable and intractable. Only a special few were aware of the inevitability of death. He was aware. He was of the special few.

"What do you suggest, Angra?"

Angra unclasped his hands and sat up. "Maybe we could reach a settlement. The first phase of the audit showed sixty thousand missing. But the break-in," he paused, inserted his finger and looked down at his desk, "that messed things up. Makes it, well, very difficult to prosecute."

"Tell you what. I'll suggest to the commissioners to settle for twenty thousand and we won't bring charges." He focused on Luke.

Luke mustered the life force that seemed to go beyond the summon and emptied it out of his eyes into Angra. Without smiling or faltering he said calmly, "I'll suggest ten thousand to Murray."

Angra could sense a final offer as well as he could tell a defendant's ability to pay a fee and this was a final offer. Despite the amount, it was exactly what he wanted. A copy of the agreement would be the perfect smear in the campaign to get Murray out of office.

"I'm sure I can persuade the commissioners to accept that," he said.

The deal was struck. Murray would pay into the county treasury ten thousand dollars, and any discrepancies in the clerk's office would be stricken. The books would start over. A new slate. Indictment would not issue against Murray. His good name prevailed. He announced shortly after negotiating the settlement he would not be a candidate for re-election. This left the race wide open for Angra's handpicked candidate, Enock Ellis.

Murray mortgaged his plantation to raise the ten thousand dollars. He soon found that rent on the plantation would not support him and make the payments. Finally he sold the plantation for one hundred thousand dollars. Murray settled with the bank, and with part of the balance he built a small house. He invested the rest to draw interest to supplement his income.

The income was meager but sufficient to purchase a black Nash automobile to chauffeur his sisters to church on Sundays and take leisurely rides in the shank of the evenings.

Murray was as devout to the church as he was to the Democratic Party, and was confident he and his sisters were going to heaven. He had never been saved by a stroke of lightning nor had God talked to him. A donation to the church, he thought, would be insurance for him to enter the pearly gates. Murray had no heirs and felt very much at ease when he executed a will leaving the residue of his estate, including his house and savings to the Methodist Church.

He signed the will with the same emotionless, wide-eyed smile he used in every transaction. The one he used when swearing a witness to tell the truth, the whole truth, and nothing but the truth.

Mary Tate

With the passing of time the sheriff's drinking increased. Sometimes he did not remember going home. Except the meals his wife occasionally prepared for him, she had little to do with him.

Mary Green Tate was a big-boned woman, well-fleshed but not fat. She had an honest, sincere, cherubic face. She sang in the choir and taught the adult Sunday School class at the First Baptist Church in the small town of Locksville. The people she associated with in church were sympathetic with regard to her husband's drinking. Although her face was strained with concern, she managed a pleasant smile when engaging in social functions.

Mary's family owned a small produce farm. She and her two sisters helped plant and harvest collards, beans, squash, okra, corn and watermelons.

Earl Tate knew how to work. He also knew how to supervise. When he was a young man, he lived near the Green family and on occasion helped Mary and her sisters with the farming.

Mary grew to admire Earl's concern, honesty, and kindness. He was courteous and quiet, and she considered him trustworthy, a man of high character and integrity. He was a member of her church and made regular donations. To her knowledge he did not drink alcoholic beverages.

Honor and security were necessary in Mary's life. Honor she thought she learned in church. She learned security in the truck farming operation. She thought Earl Tate could provide both.

They married when he became deputy, and shortly afterward they built a small house in Locksville, financed by the Farmers Home Administration.

Earl was deputy for six years before he became sheriff. During that time, Mary never smelled alcohol on his breath. His consumption of alcohol was negligible, occurring only at functions which men attended.

Shortly after he assumed the sheriff's duties, Mary began to detect the odor of alcohol on him. She did not raise the issue, because, she reasoned, the stress of the job allowed for some discrepancies. One night he came home intoxicated. This, she observed, began to occur more frequently. Mary tried to feed him properly, and comfort him. He did not respond. His drinking steadily increased.

She decided her husband was sick. He refused her suggestion that he get treatment, and she decided to manage her life the best she could and leave him to his sickness.

Mary appeared stoic to the outside world and grew impervious to him. This was the only way she could survive. Her security now was simply in waiting. Didn't the Bible teach patience, fortitude, and grace?

She finally convinced herself she was pure again and refused sex with him because she thought the Bible taught it was wrong to have sex with a drunken man. Mary slipped unconsciously into a sullen and unsullied overseer of her household.

Al's Fire

"Boys, hold up. Let's stop here a minute and see if he will do anything. He's bound to do something directly," the sheriff said. He turned and looked down the road. The others paused and wiped sweat and rain from their faces. The sheriff pulled his pint of Little Brown Jug from his pocket, drank, tossed the bottle to the edge of the road, turned and faced the house.

"Take another look, Greg," he said, his voice wavering.

"Think we're close enough, Sheriff?" Luke asked.

"I believe this is close enough. Boys, push the car to the side of the road so it will face the house broadside," the sheriff said.

"Wonder why we ain't heard from him. Reckon he's

still in there?" Greg asked.

A cloud crossed between the men and the house. It pounded the earth in milky thunder and passed quickly into the woods. The sun blazed back in a metallic silver across the roof of the house.

"I don't know," the sheriff said. "He was in there awhile ago. At least I thought he was. I thought that's what I was looking at."

They wiped the sweat and rain from their foreheads and stared at the house.

Al Jackson's eyes were fixed on the house.

"I thought I heard a back door open and close awhile ago." Luke said.

"He could have gone out the back door and gone into the forest," he added.

He wished he had. Luke wished Burge would somehow evaporate, escape the world, and never be seen again. *Craziness just does not mix with sanity. It short-circuits into itself and its energy is never used. Like the course of lightning in the sky.*

When insanity short circuits there is nothing left. The power shorts out within itself. So the insane man joins his unconsciousness to his consciousness. Insanity mixes the primitive with the civilized. It mixes the real with the unreal, the dream with reality. When that happens there is nothing left. Only ashes.

What happens when they shoot my brain with radium? I feel a melodious heat swirling in my head. Is it shorting the protons and neurons leaving nothing, not even ashes? Because that which was yesterday is not time. It has no ashes. It has no thoughts, no feeling, no substance. Nothing but the traces of is, pumping itself full of itself, not even repairing its errors. Ashes are the traces of is.

So the radium makes me ashless. Filling the static void. Because I feel it damming the flow of life, the is, the thought, the feeling. It makes me isless without creating ashes.

I hope he has escaped. I hope he is in the impenetrable forest.

"Okay, Al. Get that horn out of the boot. I'm going to try to get him to come out. That's the best way. If we can get him to come out it will be the best." The sheriff spoke as if he were arguing to a jury for a verdict in his favor.

Al went to the trunk of the car, opened it, took out the megaphone and handed it to the sheriff.

The sheriff went to the side of the cruiser which faced the house and spoke through the horn. "Wardell! Can you hear me?"

The words were friendly. Spoken to retain friendship. He had know Wardell's family since before he became deputy. Burge's family had supported him each time he ran for sheriff.

Sheriff Tate felt there came a time when justice overrode politics, especially when the injustice was a direct affront to the white women of the county and the state. He hated the job of bringing in Wardell, but it had to be done with few complications.

"Come on out, Wardell!" The sheriff called, his voice pleading, quavering.

The men were in position. Greg was leaning across the hood, aiming his rifle toward the house. Al stood at the rear of the car holding his shotgun in a present-arms position. Luke stood next to the sheriff holding his shotgun in the crook of his arm as if he were quail hunting.

Burge stirred the shucks as he moved toward the window with his twenty-two caliber rifle. He peeped through the crack in the curtain.

The shucks have quit talking and crying. Burge doesn't have to cry anymore. The animals have stopped. They have lost their legs. They cannot move. Their legs are under their bodies like panthers fixing to leap. The animals have turned into one huge white animal with its legs curled under it. It is not a whale or a shark. It is a huge white dog with glinting eyes. His feet are black, tucked under him. He is going to jump and come and eat me and mama alive. His teeth shine in the sunlight. What is he waiting for?

The sheriff spoke again, his voice booming across the yard. "Wardell! Are you in there? If you are, come out! All we want to do is take you to the doctor. The doctor will help you."

Dogs growl before they jump. He is growling. He is getting ready to jump and get me.

Luke thought, all God's chill'uns, all God's chill'uns,

and suddenly he remembered last night and he saw his wife consoling him as he sat passively drinking bourbon.

The moving finger writes, he mused, as his wife rubbed his shoulders, and having writ moves on. All your wit nor piety can lure it back to cancel half a line nor all your tears wash away a word of it.

I'm in there as well. I'm here as well. We're all God's children. The only things of value between life and the finality of death are belief and hope and trust. I believe and trust and hope. I hope Burge is not in the house. I hope he is in the forest.

"I'm going to call you one more time, Burge! Come on out now and give yourself up and we'll take you to the doctor," the sheriff shouted.

The men waited for the words to settle in the house. Luke imagined them flying around like little birds searching for nest.

"You can beat this thing." Luke's wife said as she kissed his forehead. He was thinking, death is the predator of life and life is the victim of death, an irrevocable dictum.

How comfortable he had been with life. He didn't have to think about it. He only had to enjoy it. Luke had worked hard to enjoy it. Undergraduate and law school and the discipline he had learned. It astounded him that he was suddenly staring into the end of it. It was incomprehensible that there was an end but the facts were there. There was something more than fact. There was the haunting, unsettling awareness that each moment of his life evaporated with the ticking of the clock, measuring life, not death. The moments of slaughtered time fell into the pool of death as they sucked life from him.

He felt the suction, the very lips of death upon his lifeblood, sealing the emptiness of his sterile present.

I hope Burge is not in the house. I hope he's in the forest.

"Okay Wardell! This is your last chance!" The sheriff's words blasted out of the horn as he swayed from side to side. "If you don't come out in ten minutes we are coming in!"

The sheriff let the horn drop to his side and limped back behind the car with his men.

"Either he ain't in there or he ain't coming out," he said. He opened the driver's side of the car and took a fresh pint out of the glove compartment. He broke the seal and took a drink. "I wish he would come on out of there. It would save us a lot of trouble," he muttered, as if talking to himself. He leaned forward and looked sideways at the house.

"Let's charge," Al said, as he faced the sheriff, then looked back at the house.

Greg Butler paced alongside the car, glancing at the sheriff. *This is really a mess. I have never seen anything like this. Is this swift and certain justice or a comedy of errors? Is it justice? Just what the hell are we doing?*

"I've looked several times and I didn't see anything. Didn't even see anything move. Reckon he's still in there?" Greg asked after a short pause.

"Dunno. Has anybody heard any doors slam or anything?" the sheriff asked.

"I thought I heard something around back awhile ago," Luke said. Hoped.

"There ain't nothing 'round there but a damn ole hog pen," Al said, hunching his shoulders.

They waited.

Burge's eye was on the crack in the curtain. He was sweating profusely. *The animal in the yard is almost dead. There is a little movement in one of its legs. It is lying down showing its white belly. Maybe it's sick, maybe it's dying.*

He held the rifle at attention on his right side.

Burge was a poor marksman. In boot camp he got passing marks because he was assigned to supplies. He never shot at the enemy; he had played soldier while in the Army. It was a game he created but did not like. It became not life to him, not real. Everything had become not real but it appeared real. Now there was nothing that wasn't real. *The big white animal is in the front yard sleeping. Or is it getting ready to jump and come in the house and eat me up?*

He stood trembling in his sweat. The flesh on his face twitched. When he moved, the shucks cried. Behind the house a sow and three pigs stretched in the glittering sun.

The sun and rain are after me, too. I can not run. There is no place to go.

Voices told him to stop preaching because the animals would not listen. The voices had turned into animals and would not listen. Now there was nothing but himself and the animals and the voices gone. Voices were hard to understand and take orders from. They jumbled and made no sense. They split him into pieces. *The animals used to be friendly. Now they are mad. Angry. They are coming to get me. I can't run.*

"Okay, Al," the sheriff said as he got out of the car and limped to the rear, "see if you can creep around the side over there next to the edge of the woods and find out if anything is going on around there on the back side."

"Right, Sheriff! I'll make my move."

Al readied his gun. He crouched and began moving catlike around the edge of the field. His eyes filled with plunder and kill. For the first he wanted to rob an individual of his dignity, his life. Al felt a cold indifference to all life except his own. He crouched, impervious to all things except that which balanced against his emotive force, Wardell Burge. It was not that he knew Burge personally. It didn't make any difference who Burge was. As far as he was concerned, Burge was everywhere.

It was the idea of Burge, who represented lawlessness and unfitness. *A nigger who parades naked before God and white women. A white man in the place of Burge would have been different but he would be killed, too, and Burge being who he is makes it easier.* All social responsibility slid away, like a snake shedding its skin. With him it was just like shooting a mad dog. Had Burge been white he would have been shooting a human. Under the conditions, to shoot anybody would be just fine. The sheriff's order was the first step to eradicate the vermin.

Burge watched.

The animal, the huge, white animal, is coming apart. He is breaking apart and creating more life with each break. It is like bread in the Bible, the Good Book, which says the bread will come apart and feed the masses. But this bread is coming apart to come and get me. To eat me. Bread has turned into a animal and is breaking into pieces to come to get me to eat me. A big white loaf is breaking apart into animals to come and get me.

When Al moved away from the edge of the woods toward the house, Burge fired. The bullet traveled high above Al's head into the trees. The hogs jumped and woofed. Crows began to caw and flee the field.

"Get to the woods!" the sheriff called.

Al did not heed. He lay flat on the ground and slipped the incendiary in his gun.

The men around the car prepared arms.

From the window Burge watched the motion.

The animal is breaking apart. He is breaking apart. He is a queen bee putting off drones. They are coming to get me. I have no room to go. Myself is not big enough to hide in.

Burge fired again. The bullet sailed high over the cruiser and dropped into the woods across the road. The men crouched behind the car.

Greg looked with his binoculars. He saw a blur, a flicker of motion.

"Can't get an eye on him. Can't see because of the curtains. Can't tell where he is until he shoots. And then he's gone. Can't tell if anybody else is in there or not," he said.

"Just hold your fire then. Don't look like he knows what he's doing. That's the way crazy people are. They don't know what they're doing."

The sheriff looked at Al. "Come on back over here, we're going to wait him out a little longer," he said.

Al inched toward the house.

Burge watched from behind the curtains. Beneath him the shucks scratched and cried around his trembling feet.

The men behind the cruiser were poised as if posing for a portrait. Al lay crouched, like a frog watching a bug.

They are dying again. The bread is dying and not living and not coming to get me to eat me. It is not bread anymore. It has turned to stone. I cannot eat stone.

"Al!" The sheriff yelled, and while moving around the rear end of the cruiser he stumbled and fell. "God dammit, I told you to come on back!" he screamed, holding himself up with his hands. Greg helped him to his feet.

The words went to Al but he did not hear them. He had sealed himself off from all things except his mission.

He was the roof between the hail and the earth.

Al would protect the earth from all intruders. Earth could not produce with hail banging from the sky. Al was the shield between justice and injustice, the protector of blind justice and he was also the executor, the man to carry out the plan of blind justice. His mission was greater than pretending. He did not pretend he did not hear the words. Al did not hear the words. Did not want to hear the words. Al was sworn to the covenant of justice and when that occurred nothing came between him and his goal. Nothing.

When the sheriff fell and screamed, Burge fired from the window and the bullet sailed high overhead, crossed the road and fell in the fallow field.

The red feather in the sheriff's hatband gleamed like a speck of blood as he turned his head to look at Al.

Burge eyed the road. *The stone is coming to life again and turning to blood. Little drops of blood. It is mixing with the stone and becoming animals again. The stones are mixing with the blood and changing into animals again. The white animal is turning into stone, into blood, and into animals again. The blood is coming to get me, to eat me up.*

"You want to storm the house?" Greg asked.

"No," the sheriff answered.

"What are we going to do, Sheriff?" Luke asked, hoping Burge would stop shooting. Hoping it would all stop.

"We're gonna wait him out. I know there ain't no

food in there. If we have to, we'll wait right here and starve him out." He looked toward Al and said, "Gimmie that horn. I'm going to see if I can't make Al hear me."

"You don't have anything to be afraid of, Sheriff. We have the outlawry proclamation. I think we can storm the house and get him with no trouble. You'll be protected," Greg said.

Greg did not know why he said that. *Maybe I just want to get this mess over because I ain't feeling right. I am getting sick on my stomach.*

The sheriff spoke through the horn. "Al! Come on back. He might get lucky and hit you. We don't want nobody hurt."

Al did not budge. He turned his wrist to see the time without moving his head. He was timing Burge's shots. The sheriff's words bounced off Al and he crouched closely to the earth.

Clouds began to break and scatter as if someone had fired buckshot into a flock of blackbirds. The sun bristled in the blue sky, glittering an incandescent, brilliant white, with spears of blue, nesting on the apex of the house.

"Do you think he heard me?" the sheriff turned to Greg who had his rifle leveled across the hood of the cruiser.

"He heard you all right," Greg answered without looking away from his rifle, adding, "In case I get Burge in my sight, you want me to take him out?"

Sheriff Tate went to the front door of the vehicle, sat, opened the glove compartment and took a drink. He gazed somberly at the house, as if pondering a deep philosophical premise. He did not like to think about anyone shooting Burge.

Capital punishment was for the judges to administer. Tate believed in it but regarded it as amputation. Like cutting part of a person off if he has cancer to save the whole body. Like a woman with breast cancer. You cut the breast off to save the rest of the body.

That's the way capital punishment was. A rotten, spoiled piece of society has to be cut off the body to save it. That's what had to be done with murderers, rapists and hardened criminals. Sometimes the disease could not run its course. If it did, it would destroy everything.

Burge has to be stopped; otherwise, I will lose my job. My career as sheriff will be over, the sheriff mused. The whites will go to the polls and vote solid and vote me out even though I carry 90 percent of the black vote. If my posse shoots Burge down like a mad dog, then the blacks will turn against me and that would end my career.

He would wait him out. He would take the long shot, and do like they do in war. He would blockade the port and in time make Burge come out either with his hands up or shooting. If he came out shooting, they were entitled to take whatever measure necessary to bring him in. Burge has to be brought in but he would do it the very best possible way.

He got out, held on to the side of the cruiser, stared at the house and responded to Greg, "No, not that way. We'll get him in time."

Luke Hampton wiped his forehead and looked at the sheriff. In spite of the sheriff's weaknesses he admired him.

The sheriff turned his head and his eyes met Luke's in a somber exchange of futility. Luke knew that the sheriff was trapped, and felt he had caused it by getting the outlawry proclamation. The proclamation would protect the sheriff, give him the right to bring Burge in by any means necessary. Luke realized the outlawry proclamation gave the sheriff the authority to act, without telling him how.

Luke understood that. He closed his mind briefly to Wardell Burge. *Tomorrow and tomorrow and tomorrow creeps toward us in its petty pace, and we hope it will replace today, renew today into a better today. But todays chew up the tomorrows as if they were bitter weeds and sting the taste buds into riling regret.*

There was a sound at the front door.

"Look out, men!" Luke shouted, "I think he's at the front door!"

The door creaked and trembled open. An elderly woman hobbled on her cane down the steps and with painstaking care made her way across the yard. She wore a homemade dress with patches of roses sewn on the front. Her bonnet covered her face and all that was visible were deep brown, penetrating eyes, blazing from beneath the hood.

"Don't shoot," she said. Her words bobbled on her voice as if coming from beneath water.

She continued to make her way toward the cruiser, hobbling with both hands on the cane.

"It's Margaret Burge, his mama," the sheriff said. "Make sure you don't do nothin' wrong," he added.

"Sheriff," she said, her voice pleading as if she were asking for her freedom, trembling as if she were coming apart.

"Don't kill 'em. He don't need killin'. He's crazy, that's what's wrong. He's been crazy a long time. Ever'body knows that. Please Sheriff, don't kill 'em."

She leaned on her cane with both hands as if trying to force the words into the earth to make them stick permanently into the world.

The sheriff, Luke, and Greg looked at her with awe. Luke and the sheriff knew every word she uttered was the truth.

It was the first time Greg had realized that the only thing they were dealing with was a crazy man. He had inflicted no physical harm to anyone. If he were going to kill a man he wanted it to be for a purpose. The whole affair suddenly seemed illogical, against the principles of God-fearing people. *This could not be in God's plan. If it were?*

"Okay, men." The sheriff looked at Al, who still lay facing the house. "And you, Al, come on back over here and let's wait him out."

Al turned and faced him with a smile and said without moving, "I'd better stay here, Sheriff, and cover you men. I ain't gonna do nothing 'til I have to. You don't know what that man's gonna do." He turned his smile back to the house.

"Is there anybody in the house besides Wardell?" the sheriff asked.

"No. Nobody but him." Margaret answered. They turned and looked at the house as if trying to will Burge to come out.

"Mrs. Burge, don't you want to sit in the car?" Greg asked.

Greg Butler did not understand why he called Margaret Mrs. Burge. His family had always called elderly colored people uncle and aunt. They were not called Mr. or Mrs., an honor they were not entitled. The words, Mrs. Burge, slipped out of him as if they were corks held underwater and had suddenly escaped.

He looked at Margaret as if she were not a stranger but an elderly woman trembling with pleas to not kill her son. It was natural. As natural as when his mother snatched him from the farm pond when he was a boy, after he had gone under for the third time.

He thought about that fleetingly as Margaret Burge turned and met his eyes with wonder, fear, and anxiety.

She did not answer, but turned her eyes to the house.

Burge peeped through a crack.

They have drawn Mama out to them. With their magnetism they have drawn Mama out to them. Are they going to eat her up?

"See if you can call him out," the sheriff said to Margaret Burge.

She cleared her voice and called, "Wardell! Wardell! Come on out. They ain't gonna hurt 'cha." Filled with desperation, she hurled the trembling words.

Her shaking hand went to her forehead and wiped sweat.

"Tell 'em we're gonna take him to the doctor," the sheriff added.

Margaret began to pant. She wavered on the cane. The sheriff braced on the front of the cruiser and looked at the house. Greg and Luke gazed at the woman.

"They're gonna take you to the doctor!" She sputtered as loudly as possible. Her back was wet with sweat. Her joints creaked.

Wardell watched from above.

They have eat her up and she has become them. Made her wrong side out and against me. They have eat her up! The big white beast has eat her up and she is white. By eating her they have turned her white and the big white animal is coming to eat me up because I can't stop them because they have turned into animals and they can't stop themselves because they are animals and animals don't stop themselves because they can't and they are coming to eat me and I can't stop them!

The shucks scuttered beneath his nervous feet.

Al Jackson watched the window.

Suddenly rifle fire spouted from the window. At the same time a muffled thump came from the source of rifle fire, as if the building had ingested something of ill portent and was attempting to belch.

When the incendiary hit Burge and exploded, pain flashed within his body and condemned it. Pain passed through and out of him, and on the same instant he flew out of himself into the flames and out the window as his body fell backward in the shucks.

Sheriff Tate reeled backward, stumbled, and fell. Greg hurriedly helped him to his feet.

"What happened?" the sheriff asked as smoke began to boil out of the second-story window.

There was a pause.

"I don't know," Greg lied. He and Luke knew that Al had fired an incendiary.

Luke remained mute.

It happened quickly. The firing of the rifle and shotgun was intertwined in such rapid sequence that it was difficult to tell the difference between the two.

Margaret Burge tried to run to the house, riding the cane as if it were a hobby horse.

"Stop it!" she screamed, falling. "Stop it!" Her hands clawed at the earth as she tried to pull herself toward the house.

Greg Butler picked her up and held her by her upper arms, steadying her.

She trembled in his hands.

"I'm having bad pain, here," she said, clutching her chest and beginning to whimper. "I'm hurtin' bad," she squeaked and clasped her hands over her chest and collapsed.

Greg eased her softly to the ground. He took off his fatigue jacket, fashioned it into a pillow and placed it gently under her head.

"I think she's having a heart attack," he said softly.

Al moved from his position and stood next to the cruiser. He smiled and spoke laconically, ignoring Margaret Burge, "You reckon the fool has set the house on fire?"

"Somebody has." Greg said.

Luke and Greg watched the smoke writhing out the windows. They felt as if something exploded inside them, rendering them helpless and they were watching the consumption of themselves spewing out.

Al stood motionless, capturing the twisting flames with his eyes, smiling.

"This is unexpected," the sheriff said. *Burge ought to come out now. With his hands up. Maybe he's got sense enough to surrender. I hope to the Lord he don't come out shooting.*

"Sheriff," Greg interrupted, "we'd better cover the

doors and windows."

"Yeah," the sheriff answered in a stupor. "Al!" he yelled, "Cover the back side! I'll stay here. Greg, you take care of Margaret and keep a look out over there.

"He pointed to the woods opposite Al. "Luke, go over there where you can see down the other side. Don't nobody shoot unless he shoots at you."

They moved into position and waited. The house boiled.

They waited.

The house boiled violently.

"I believe she's having a heart attack, Sheriff," Greg said louder, cautiously observing Margaret's pain-stricken face.

"God damn! What can go wrong next?" the sheriff asked as he stumbled to the cruiser.

He barely heard Margaret mutter haltingly, "Don't kill 'em, don't kill 'em, he ain't nothing but crazy."

A twinge of terror ran through Greg. He briefly pictured a butterfly flying within him searching for flower blooms. Felt the search as the butterfly flapped softly. He shook. The sheriff opened the door to the cruiser, fell butt-first on the seat and began keying the transmitter.

"This is Sheriff Tate! This is Sheriff Tate! We have a house on fire, a bad fire! Down the Catfish Lake Road. Yeah, on the Catfish Lake Road! A woman has had a heart attack, too! This is a real bad emergency. Send the rescue squad, too." He keyed again and waited.

A voice squawked back. "On the Catfish Lake Road?"

"Yeah. The Catfish Lake Road," the sheriff mumbled. "Come fast," he added, "it's a bad one."

Luke watched the fire licking through the windows, hoping Burge would come out with his hands up.

He shuddered silently and felt the flames flowing through him, out of his belly and heart. It was a hollow feeling, with no pain or joy. Helplessly, purposelessly ravaging his body, his feelings, like the cancer in his head. He imagined the fire fueling out of him, carrying the cinders in an onrush, leaping upward, becoming light feathery ashes and descending like angels through the clarity of the sky.

A black cloud rushed overhead and threatened rain, then disappeared over the woods.

The silver sun returned, blazing through the smoke.

Margaret Burge lay with her eyes closed and her arms folded over her chest.

"Are you hurting bad?" Greg asked.

She continued to pant, her mouth turned down in fixed resolve. "Bad," she barely uttered.

"Hold on. The rescue squad will be here soon." Greg said.

Flames burst through the roof. Timbers began to break and fall.

Luke imagined the flames consuming his flesh, baking it into cinders which disappeared into the sky. Now his bones were in the kiln. They were breaking because they refused to burn. They were clacking against each other and the flames. There would be something left. Bones and ashes. The ashes had separated and gone into the sky and returned as delicate angels. The bones remained stubborn and recalcitrant. Broken, but not destroyed.

He moved to the front of the cruiser and took the bottle from the glove compartment and drank. He drank again and it was empty. The fire rushed through him again and for a moment time stopped. As he turned and looked at the house, now wearing a crown of leaping and twisting red and black hair, he knew that only one thing stopped time. That only death had the power to stop time once. Only once.

He's not going to come out. Burge doesn't want to come out. He is going to stop time. For one brief second between motion and stasis, life and death, that time of commitment that hews definitions and separates all things unto themselves. Burge will make that mark.

Omar was right. The moving finger writes and having writ, moves on. Having writ, time stops. So there is nothing left but the writing. When the writing stops there is nothing left except the ashes. There are no tears to put out the fire because the tears cannot come during the fire, they must come after, and after is always too late. I wish I had a tear. If I had, it would be for nought. Erase nothing but time, and to erase time is destruction.

His eyes swelled but did not leak. He heard the sirens from the fire trucks and ambulance moaning in the distance like creatures mortally wounded.

The fire raged like boiling blood. It had decapitated the house, and the walls began collapsing inward. The fire trucks, bearing down the road, flashing frantically for clearance, issued more blasts of pain and mourning, which mixed with the anger of the fire.

Outside the tumult surrounding him, Luke heard a distant rumble. He thought it was his soul. Luke had never heard his soul before. Had never seen it. He had never given his soul much thought. Something mentioned casually in philosophy classes and sometimes his minister would bring man's soul into his sermons. It was a seldom mentioned abstraction, and abstractions had no substance.

Now he was sure he heard it. The distant rumble was the disgruntled rumble of man attempting civilization, administering justice in his crusade to identify himself. It rumbled out of the caveman's mouth and off his club, through the witch doctor's jig, through the secular pride of the earliest clans. It rumbled through the clashing of swords, the arrow's sting, the bullet's velocity and the explosion of bombs; from every jail cell, every rape and robbery and murder, and through the chains of slavery and exploitation, through every emotion and self-righteous urge that directed man's course.

There ought to be tears before things happen. Even before happiness. There are tears. Many tears trying to recycle joy and happiness and many trying to wash away the bitter rewards of man's drive for identity.

The ambulance arrived with the fire trucks which posted positions around the house, as if holding it hostage. The firemen faced an inferno.

Greg Butler rushed to the driver's side of the ambulance and shouted, "The woman is over here!" His voice rose above the roar of the engines, leaping, subduing the violence of the flames.

He pointed to his left. "She's having a heart attack and needs help bad!"

He opened the door for the driver and helped take out the carrier.

"Anybody in there?" the fire chief shouted.

The sheriff stumbled to him and said. "There was. We think there was. We don't know. He might have left the back way. We hope so."

"Yeah, she's having a heart attack," the attendant confirmed, after checking her blood pressure and heartbeat.

"Did'ja kill'em? Did'ja kill'em?" Margaret rasped as Greg and the attendant lifted her onto the carrier and carried her to the ambulance.

Al Jackson stood beside the sheriff. He held his gun in the crook of his arm, as if he had just won a skeet-shooting contest. "It must be pure lightwood," he said, "Look at that damn thing burn. If he is in there, he ain't coming out."

Luke and the sheriff turned and stared at him, but Al

did not take his eyes from the raging flames.

A single cloud drifted and split in the distance as the last flames flickered and died under the force of the fire hoses.

Luke, Greg, the sheriff and Al had already smelled the burning flesh, pungent and repugnant. They looked into the debris as if the waste, the terrible residue, were going to issue a condemnation.

The firemen picked through the debris. Smoke curved in apparitions as it rose weightless from the ashes.

The house was destroyed, leaving part of the walls standing, variegated and stark, as if surrounding a crater formed by a meteorite.

"Here's something over here," the fire chief said, prodding next to a partially destroyed wall.

The sheriff held onto Luke and the three men walked toward the fireman.

Al pulled his cap down and stared under the brim at the four men.

Burge lay on his back, partially covered with ashes, his arms stretched beside him. His charred flesh was partially washed from his bones by the firemen's hose. He looked as if, after being buried many years, time had wasted the earth from around him and pulled the flesh from his bones. Sunlight sparkled brilliantly and dimmed in the pools of water that stood in his eye sockets.

He lay like a mummy, grim, buried without a casket

and unswaddled, rising through the ashes of time and speaking, voiceless, ancient words of dishonor.

"I reckon that's Burge," the sheriff said.

Al Jackson helped carry the remains of Wardell Burge to the ambulance. Smiling sardonically, he gave the carrier its final push. The siren screamed as the ambulance tore into the distance."There's got to be a report filled out," the sheriff said. "But we can do that tomorra'. There's nothing else to do around here. Al, you can get ready to drive us to the courthouse if you want to, and then you can go on home." The sheriff lost balance and fell against the cruiser.

Luke was sitting on the passenger side of the cruiser with the door open. His feet were resting on the ground.

Greg Butler was restless and depressed. He felt he had been in the midst of a huge explosion and was left standing in the hollow of its remains. Any place on earth was better than where he was. For the first time in his life he felt completely out of joint with law enforcement. Mission accomplished. Wardell Burge cornered, and the issue settled. Justice did prevail, even if it was radical.

"Mr. DA" he said, standing aside from the others, "Do you think you'll be needing me any more?"

"No," Luke answered. "We're going back to the courthouse now. You can go on home from there."

Frances Jackson

Al Jackson was full of himself as he drove from the courthouse home. He was the hero, he knew he was. The others resented him because he had the nerve, the guts, to eradicate the monster. Al was convinced it galled Greg Butler because Greg was the man who was supposed to do the deed. He upstaged Greg and Greg was sick. He could tell. That was too bad. Now he could plan on running for sheriff. The Klan would be 100 percent behind him. A solid white vote would beat a solid black vote anytime in Ownes County.

Al liked the smell of the burned wood, shucks, corn, and flesh on his clothes. He breathed deeply, concentrating on the scent, savoring every particle as if he were enjoying a gourmet meal.

Amy would not like the smell. He would take a bath and change into his clean uniform. To him the smell was almost like the smell of sex. Violent, earthy and intoxicating. Finally, he felt secure. He had killed a man.

"What is that awful smell?" Frances asked when he entered the house.

"We had a fire," he answered through tight lips, "and we got our man."

"Well, hurry up and get out of those clothes and clean up. You know we've got to eat early tonight. I've got bridge club, you know."

They usually ate a sandwich Wednesday nights. Al made prevention calls. That is what he told her. The sheriff had created the prevention patrol, and Al was it. He patrolled the hot spots of the county to keep domestic violence in hand. He was doing a good job, too. Wife-beating had gone down to practically nothing. Seldom did a wife shoot her husband, and if it did happen that didn't count. Most of the niggers beating niggers they didn't investigate because they needed beating. Al always laughed and adjusted his gun belt as he spoke those words.

Frances was content to teach school. She was not interested in establishing new teaching principles nor promoting social advancement for any of her students.

Her sexual activity with Al was at her whim and was erratic and unpredictable. She had more headaches than time for sex. When she did call upon Al for his services, she was like an animal, consumed by the drive for reproduction. During those times Al would accuse her of being in heat. This diluted his own desires because she became the aggressor and dominated him in the process. He didn't like domination of any sort.

Al's father, Dewey, was an expert ditch digger. He took pride in digging straight and well-shaped ditches. Most farmers needed small drainage lines dug through low spots in their fields. Dewey chewed tobacco and dug, sometimes twelve hours a day.

Al was ashamed of his father's work. He wanted to do better. After he finished high school, he became active in the fire and rescue squad. While working as a filling station attendant, he went to community college at night and studied law enforcement and criminal justice. When the sheriff's deputy resigned to take a job on the police force in Jacksonville, Al applied for and got the job. Tate liked his credentials.

Al dated Frances during his senior year in high school. They were on the basketball teams and traveled together. Al gave his undivided attention to her and they became serious daters. She liked him because she thought he looked up to her and she controlled the relationship.

When she graduated from college and returned home, he was deputy sheriff and they married. He was in bliss, and she had a husband.

"Do you have any place special you're going tonight?" she asked as she took a bite from her sandwich.

"No. Just routine," he answered as he chewed.

They ate silently and when she stood to leave she said, "I'll be coming in early tonight. See if you can come in a little early."

She tidied her dress as she stood and smiled and raked her hands down her stomach.

"If something don't come up, I will," he said and smiled faintly as he took the last bite of bread.

Robert Killingsworth

Robert Killingsworth watched from the bushes. He moved his head furtively, like a weasel, as he peeped through the dog fennels.

The cicadas rattled the air and he thought about a symphony of violins. He smelled the strong fragrance and felt the soft tender blooms. Robert was cool and nervous in the evening air. The night breathed through a faint breeze. He opened his mouth and took a deep breath. Robert thought he was eating the darkness. He looked to the stars and thought they would drop as spears of tears.

The house sat across the road.

Robert had walked from his trailer. Initially he would

drive by and look. He had driven by often and looked. He stopped after the deputy sheriff's car began parking in the driveway.

There was a revulsion in him about the deputy he did not understand. It was not because of Amy, yet it was. Robert cared for her enough to marry her when he came home from the war.

The war did something to him. It killed courage. Killed honor and respect. Killed the killer in him. He came home not wanting to kill again.

He went in the Navy at eighteen as a volunteer. He was assigned to a landing craft, and it was his job to drive the soldiers to the beach.

"When you get to the beach and let the ramp down, if any of them refuse to go ashore, shoot them," the captain had said.

The third time he went ashore the water was churning with dead boys. Dead boys littered the shoreline. The sky was falling with dangling boys. His sea craft was filled with crying boys.

When the ramp went down, the soldiers refused to move. No one moved to leave the craft. They began to shake and cry. There was no place to go. Pulling his rifle up, he could not shoot, but he could cry. There was no honor in crying. He stopped crying and backed the craft up with the ramp down. Water rushed in and the boys waded as fast as they could to the shore. He followed them.

Robert fell and hid behind the dead boys until the men advanced across the hill. The air filled with sound and fire.

When the beachhead cleared, he contacted an Army man who radioed his ship and his unit sent for him. He reported his boat as hit and sunk. They believed him.

After that, he was no good in the war. Robert stayed in the hospital until they gave him a medical discharge and sent him home.

Robert wondered if he would cry tonight. Crying didn't sound good with the cicadas and frogs and the whippoorwill and owls. He heard a mourning dove behind him.

Every Wednesday night for the past six months he had been coming to watch. He could see forms inside the bedroom. Robert was jealous of Al doing something he couldn't do. After the war he froze up. That is the way he felt. After the whore in St. Louis he decided against whores. There was something about prostitution that was like an animal—wild and plundering.

The doctor said, "You will have to take this medicine the rest of your life. Nerves. It's your nerves and you don't cure nerves. War jitters, shell shock, whatever you call it, that's what you have."

Shame roomed with his nerves. When they entangled, he flushed and felt helpless and naked. That was the way he was most of the time.

Robert met Amy at a veterans benefit dinner. She was

friendly and he liked her. Her husband was killed in the war and she was sympathetic toward veterans. She thought she could help him, thought she could soothe his nerves. They married and bought a house through the Veterans Administration.

Sex came rarely, only after Amy spent considerable time soothing, stimulating and arousing him. Shame and nerves interfered. The time eventually came when there was no sex. Shame built upon itself and entangled his nerves. Robert and Amy began to argue and he became helpless. They did not pass blows nor did he threaten her. The arguments became more frequent and finally they slept in different bedrooms.

That is when he became interested in guns. He had forgotten the guns in service. Their purpose. Now, he was not interested in killing nor hunting, but began to love to fondle pistols. He received a sense of power he could not understand merely by touching and holding them.

Firing them in target practice, he gained a greater sense of power through the explosion and force in his hand. The scars on the targets were after the fact, a happenstance of the feeling. While he was handling a pistol or firing it, his nerves disappeared.

Amy's face became taut. She never told him to leave, nor volunteered to leave. Robert saw the tightness and frightened look. He knew he was causing it and decided to move out.

Robert had never tried to explain love, to himself or anyone else. He didn't know enough about it to discuss it. Amy asked him if he loved her. He said he didn't know. She said she loved him and he believed it. That was his experience with love.

Medical disability payments allowed him to save enough money to buy a house trailer with some to spare. Robert bought the trailer and gave Amy the remainder of the savings and had half his check sent to her. He felt good that he was helping her.

He did not know why he remained attracted to Amy, nor did he think about it. It was a feeling that swelled inside him, causing him to do things he did not understand. Like watching from the weeds and bushes. He detested the whole thing yet there he was. It caused his nerves to jump all over him and put him in spasms. Al Jackson was credited with that.

Al was late tonight. Usually he came shortly after eight as the sun was setting in summer and after the news during the winter.

Perhaps he went to the fire down the Catfish Lake Road. It was a bad fire. Robert saw the smoke filling the sky from his yard while he was target practicing and he saw it later, on the news. It looked like a mean fire. Mean fires to Robert were like the fires coming out of the battleships, artillery, tanks, and planes. Warfire, he called it, but never said it to anyone else. He was afraid to because he was afraid of war and you were not supposed to be afraid of war.

He stirred in the dog fennels and smelled them. The cicadas and frogs rattled the quick of his being. A door opened on the front porch and Amy came out and looked up and down the road and listened for the sound of a car. The porch light was a single bulb hanging from the center of the ceiling.

As if summoned, a car came around the bend. Al's cruiser. Its headlights burned the night like eager, yellow eyes. The car approached quickly, faster than usual and stopped abruptly in front of the house. Al bounded to the porch.

"I barbecued me a nigger today," he bragged.

This infuriated Robert. He did not know what Al was talking about but he sensed it was bad wrong.

Al grabbed Amy and kissed her hard and said, "My blood is boiling tonight. I believe I'm gonna run for sheriff. I'm gonna give it to you right tonight." He jerked her inside.

The moon was rising full, overwhelming the stars. Crickets began to chirp, mixing with the cicadas and frogs. An incessant chattering mixing with Robert's nerves. All the sounds around him became wild and vibrant, a strident plea for freedom.

The moon was to his back and struck full on the bedroom window. Al raised the window and stuck his head out and listened. The two-way radio in his car squawked and scratched. He never wanted to lose contact with the central nervous system of the law. Communications and the fire from a gun were the blood of the law to him. Wherever he parked his cruiser, he left his radio on. Robert Killingsworth shuddered when Al pulled off his gun belt and hung it on the bedpost. The handle of the three-fifty-seven magnum hung like a bull horn from its holster. Billy sticks stuck out like knives stove to the hilt. Al moved to the other side of the bed and began taking off his clothes and hanging them on the other bedpost. A chill ran Robert into a corner of himself and he felt submerged in a chamber so cold he could not imagine it on earth. He felt naked and ashamed.

Amy lay nude, like a wax figure, as if her flesh had melted and poured into a mold. She was a light walnut color.

"I've already started one fire today and lo and behold I'm called to put one out." Al chuckled.

"What are you talking about, you barbecued a Negro? What kind of talk is that?"

"It's a long story. That nigger down on the Catfish Lake Road. That crazy that's been preaching naked and stopping the U.S. mail and scaring people to death down there. Let me put this fire out and then I'll tell you all about it."

He mounted her.

"The sheriff was drunk and made a mess out of the whole thing. I had to take over and get the job done.

The sheriff needs to step down and let me take over." The words jerked out of him with his body motion.

"Don't talk while you're doing this," she said.

As Robert witnessed the inscrutable interpossession of bodies unraveling and entwining, each striving passionately to overpower the other, an unimaginable heat consumed him. Its seat was in his consciousness. It boiled out of his head and poured like molten lava, flowing inexorably, covering and consuming his flesh and his awareness. He felt he could not endure it. Robert closed his eyes and nothing left him. He slowly opened his eyes and his nerves began singing again with an onrush of every insecurity and shame he had ever experienced.

Without thinking, he got on his knees and crawled toward the window. The radio crackled and scratched. He heard noises from the room, unintelligible male and female utterances, gasping for breath and the expelling of air. Bed springs squeaked in a primitive, emergent rhythm.

When he reached the house, he slowly rose until he could see inside.

Amy's pale, walnut colored body lay beneath Al. Her legs were over his shoulders. He was kissing her on the neck. Her eyes were closed and she was moaning in a primitive unraveling of her psyche—painful, esoteric, and amatory.

This was the first time Robert had dared go to the

house since he left it. He stared, and felt a hot urgency flood his being. It was not only in his flesh but in his mind. His nerves ran hot as if tiny lightning bolts were racking his body, and strange anger seized him as he felt a tiny throb grow into an erection. His erection nudged against the pistol he carried in his pocket for protection.

Tears began to stream down his face. That was the first time he had known tears since his boat sank. He had cried since, but it was only a noise. No tears came.

Al's body began to jerk with spasmodic orgasm. Robert began to sob and tremble, and Amy turned her head and saw him.

It was as if a bodiless, innocent face appeared like an apparition and sat on the window sill before her. His pale blue eyes opened wide and absorbed what he felt to be the shameful disgrace of his life.

At first Amy's mouth opened as if to swallow something vile and incomprehensible, or as if she was looking at a ghost. Then her mouth tightened and her face twisted with the agony of her scream.

Al turned his head and faced, with an unbelievable sense of terror and finality, the rushing explosion of a German Luger.

The bullet struck Al in the middle of his forehead and exited the back of his head, splattering Amy with blood. As his body quivered in the final phase of orgasm, she wiggled herself from beneath him and cowered in the corner, still screaming. The scream started a split second before the bullet struck, muffling the expanding force of the pistol shot. It recouped its force as the sound of the shot ceased and split forth, fearfully spiraling in a peal of anguish.

Robert straightened up on cold columns of air and walked stiffly across the field. The moon hung, high and crystal, like a single frozen tear. He was conscious only of his cold and nerveless body.

He walked to the road and headed home, amazed that his body felt so cold and pure. So steady and calm. No longer did the cicadas and crickets rattle his nerves. Impervious to everything except his awareness that he was trying to feel, he felt absolutely nothing except the cold walking cylinder he had become.

There wasn't the chill running his backbone, which he so often felt, not so much as a single thought seized his brain, not so much as a want for a single thing.

Behind him, Amy's peal of anguish continued unabated, rising in intensity and pitch. It hung in the sky behind him as if her soul had been ripped from her and put to sound.

He continued, unhearing, moving with long, cold, swift strides until he reached his home. He walked into his house, and with mechanical dexterity dialed the sheriff's office.

Tate's Disease

Sheriff Earl Tate was alone, feeling as if a terrible storm had passed and he was in its core. Exhausted, he received the call.

"I killed that deputy of yours at Amy's house. This is Robert Killingsworth. Just done it." The words exploded in his mind in violent eruptions as if shot out of a pistol. The world Earl Tate had created for himself subdued and muffled the impact, as if the explosions were under water.

The diseases were out of control.

Thin slits in the sheriff's awareness opened with each word Robert uttered and cut through his protective veil. Through the slits he felt the diseases pouring swiftly, violently, into his spirit, feeding ravenously, emptying him as if he were their royal meal.

He tried to call back. There was no answer. At Amy's house there was no answer. He called Al's house. There was no answer. Earl Tate went to his cruiser and keyed his transmitter for Al's cruiser. He received nothing but static. Then he called for help.

"This is Sheriff Tate. I think I'm going to need an ambulance out at Amy Killingsworth's. Not sure, but think so."

"We got one vehicle left," the dispatcher said, "The other one took Burge's mama to the hospital."

"Don't want to take no chances. Send one on out there. I'm on my way now."

The sheriff heard the screaming as he got out of his cruiser. He entered the room and found the body lying with the face toward him. Tate stared at Al. A bullet hole was directly above the bridge of the nose in the middle of the forehead. Eyes were open and fixed in recognition of the final horror of extinction, written at the moment of explosion.

Amy was in the corner on her hands and knees, naked, screaming. Her eyes were closed. Her face twisted with the trauma of violence beyond her comprehension or ability to feel.

Through the years, the sheriff had developed an invincibility that enabled him to appear unmoved at anything. He had witnessed a few mutilated bodies and the aftermath of several gory suicides, but this scene rattled him.

He stood mute as the rescue squad pulled into the yard.

Glenn Privet and Alice Byrd, hearing the screaming, rushed in with the carrier.

"What the hell happened?" Glenn asked.

"I don't know," the sheriff answered.

Glenn and Alice hurriedly went to the bed, rolled the body over and began checking for vital signs.

"What a damn mess," Glenn swore as Alice threw a sheet over Amy.

"There are no vital signs," he said. He pulled a sheet over the body and turned to Amy. "God! She's in bad shape!"

The sheriff limped around them as they worked. When they drove away, the sound of the siren and the hum of the engine churned in his mind in a hapless call to his spirit.

"Damn," he said to himself.

Then he went to Robert's house.

When the sheriff entered, Robert stared at him cold and emotionless.

"This is what I did it with," he said, mechanically extending the pistol butt-first. The sheriff accepted the Luger and dropped it into his coat pocket.

"Why did you do it, Robert?" the sheriff asked.

Robert continued to stare at him with that vacuous

indifference used for responding to questions that have no answers. He knew only that there was a wellspring within him that refused to respond. The nakedness and shame he once felt had vanished.

The disease, the sheriff thought, as he stared at Robert. Another disease has run its course.

"If you don't know, I don't know." That was all Robert said when the district attorney and the sheriff asked him in the holding room.

"If you don't know, I don't know," was the answer he gave the panel of psychiatrists at Dorothea Dix Hospital.

"He is not competent to stand trial," the chief medical examiner said after an extensive examination.

"He should be committed until we determine him competent to stand trial," the doctors finally said.

After three days at Neuse Memorial Hospital, Amy Killingsworth refused to take food or medicine. Her screaming had retreated into a whimpering wheeze that exhausted her breath as quickly as she drew it in. Now they were giving her shots whenever necessary to put her to sleep and feeding her intravenously. She had not uttered a word since the pistol shot. The doctors had no choice except to send her to Dorothea Dix Hospital.

Luke's Prayer

Luke poured bourbon over ice and sat at the kitchen table. His face had a pinkish-plum cherubic glow, which belied the heavy uncertainties filling his being. He felt glutted with thick, immovable blackness. He was to himself a black hole turned inside out.

Beverly smelled the smoke and acrid scent of burnt wood, shucks, corn, and flesh on his clothes.

"What happened?" she asked sitting opposite him.

"We burned him up." Luke answered with leaden words.

His face hung fixed, emotionless, waiting for something to happen. Then it hit him. The feeling that nothing was ever going to happen. If something happened, it would be too late and it would be the last. It was a disaster waiting for something to happen and knowing it would be the last thing that would happen. He was on a crazy turnstile sitting squarely on the pivot of time.

"How could you burn him up?"

"That crazy deputy."

"What?"

"We burned him up." Luke looked past Beverly out the window. His arm moved the glass, like a robot, to his mouth and as he drank, the ice cubes jingled in small, fragile tinkles.

"Burned him? That's a strange thing to happen."

"That crazy deputy."

Beverly stood behind him and rubbed his shoulders. Luke raised his glass and drank.

"I could talk about it and talk about it and it would still be the same," he said.

It's the moving finger again. Now the bird of time is on the wing and has but a short distance to fly.

Beverly continued to rub his shoulders.

"I think I want a ham and cheese sandwich. That's all I want." He drank again and the cubes tinkled sharply against the glass.

Beverly turned to the refrigerator and took out the ham and cheese.

"You sure this is all you want?" she asked.

"That's all."

After he showered and Beverly lay passively next to him in bed, he considered the good life he had enjoyed. Up to now there had been no death. There had been only life. He and his wife fitted into a clichéd society that moved toward tomorrow, filling days with moments of anticipation and expectation, propelling him to his next step, governor.

It came so easily, the soft wind in his schooner's sails. The bourbon and medium rare steaks with friends in his yard overlooking the sound. Attending the various bar meetings where he and the judges were honored guests. The always available, quiet beauty that lay in Beverly's attendance.

These things passed through his mind as if he had pulled the handle of a slot machine and the oranges and bars and grapes and lemons and cherries and plums cascaded, clicking, one-two-three, and he was afraid to look to see whether one lemon or three bells had stopped.

Then he tried to pray. *Please, Lord. Please, Lord. Forgive me, Jesus. I know that I have not... I have always neglected... Give me one more chance. I pledge that if...* Luke continued to make words, and they flew out of him like wingless birds falling into a pitiless dark.

He felt a giant vacuum growing within him as the words left. Luke felt abandoned. More poignantly, he felt as if he had abandoned himself. He lay in the darkness watching himself flying off and falling into the depthless blackness of despair. He hacked himself apart with words and sent them out, wingless, into the blackness of eternity's breath.

Then there arose from within the pit created by the frantic expulsion of his words, a word so dense, so indestructibly hard, so mighty in weight, so unimaginable in lightness, so soft in expression, so mysterious in meaning, so glorious in being, that he closed his eyes and understood nothing except that he existed, because of something else.

"God," he said. "God. God. God. God."

And then he slept.

The next day from his office he called Judge Moore.

"Judge, I think we have a problem. A fool deputy in the posse shot an incendiary into the house yesterday and burned Burge up when we went for him."

"Did the sheriff call for him to surrender?"

"Yes, he did."

"Well, you are all right, then."

They paused. The judge waited for Luke to say, that's right. You're right. Everything is okay.

Luke said, "Burge was never charged with a crime. There was never a criminal warrant issued against him. His conduct was due to him being crazy. The outlawry proclamation stated he held the congregation of Myrtle Grove Church hostage and that he terrorized people on the road. There was no criminal warrant against him. The people of the church refused to press criminal charges against him. They said he was doing crazy things because he was crazy, not because he was a criminal. We couldn't get a single one of them to bring criminal charges."

Pausing, Luke listened into the phone, then continued, "The law says that if a person is accused of a felony, then an outlawry proclamation can be issued. Certainly the petition accused him of a felony. This should protect the sheriff from any wrongdoing."

He hesitated, then said haltingly, "there's another thing, Judge. His mama was in that house."

"For God's sake! Was she burned?"

"No, but she had a heart attack after she came out of the house."

"How is she now?"

"She's in the hospital in the intensive care unit. The bad thing is the last words she used when they were putting her in the ambulance was 'Did'ja kill'em, did'ja kill'em, you don't haf'ta kill'em, he don't need killin', he ain't nothing but crazy, that's all'."

The judge waited.

"Judge," Luke continued, "There's something else. That fool deputy who fired the incendiary was murdered within four hours of the fire."

A long pause followed while nothing but breathing passed down the phone lines.

Finally the judge said, "You'd better hold a coroner's inquest. How well does the sheriff know the coroner?"

"I'm sure he knows him real good."

"Then you better move and move fast."

That afternoon Luke called the sheriff. "Talked to Judge Moore. He said we ought to have a coroner's inquest. I agree. How well do you know the coroner?"

"I can handle him okay."

"All right then. Try to lay off the bottle and let's speed things up."

Greg's Choice

When Greg Butler left Ownes County, the sun lay like a silver crown in the west. He lived east of Clayton in Johnston County, seventy miles northwest of Hamlet. He could drive that distance in little over an hour. Today he didn't. Greg wanted to be home, yes, but today he took his time, relaxing at the wheel and thinking about past events.

Greg pondered finding his friend Gene in the woods with his throat slit. The terrible look of fixed resignation Gene wore in death, having died because of a murderer-at-large. Good killed by evil. He remembered feeling good during the whole process of capturing the murderer, bringing him to trial and seeing him executed.

Now, he no longer felt good about the execution of the murderer. Felt as if he had swallowed a hard rock and it lay in the pit of his stomach. It would not digest and pass. That hard rock represented his childhood and the dogma of his preacher-father. His father, a lay preacher who had a sermon ready at every opportunity, offered the rigid word of God, never to mean anything except exactly what it said. God's law was the law. There was no other.

Greg was now thinking and feeling that there was another law and it was definitely man's law. Man could not execute God's law here on earth to carry out His mandates. First, man violated God's law when he murdered and stole. Then, in the name of justice, he murders. So, murder begets murder, rape begets rape, crime begets crime. There is only one way for man to live and that is for each individual to loosen the ties with crime and evil in the solitude of his or her own being and let God do the rest. Let God do his doings without the interference of man.

Margaret was as well as dead. What kind of justice would take her life? Burge. What kind of justice took his?

When Greg drove into his yard, the sun rested in a silver splash on his windshield. It was near this time each evening, unless there was an emergency, when he came home. His children, Greg Jr. and Mary, always rushed to greet him. He would pat them on the head and sometimes brusquely hug them as they clung to his rigid legs. They wanted to jump in his arms. Although he had them under firm control, he felt they were alien creatures. Pieces of property life had given him.

When he got out of his car and started toward the house, the children rushed toward him. Spontaneously, he dropped to one knee. He had never done that. Always it was the pat, pat, pat on the head and the brisk, distant hug.

When they came around him, his head was equal in height to Greg Jr.'s and taller than Mary's. They wrapped him with the tenderness of their arms and hands and buried their faces with touching against each side of his. He had never been aware of the soft, innocent tenderness of his children's touch and flesh. The miracle of the child moved him and as they melted into each other, he felt the trickle of tears slowly descend his face.

"Daddy! Daddy! You smell like fire!" The words swelled out of the children around him like butterflies around a flower as he held tightly, tenderly, their pliant bodies.

"Have you been to a fire, Daddy?"

Greg Butler, gathering the children to his body, one in each arm, rose to his feet and headed to the house. He felt he had become a fruit tree and had ripped his roots from the earth and, laden with fruit, become mobile.

His wife waited on the steps.

"Yes," he said softly, "I've been to a fire."

"Tell us about it, Daddy, tell us about it!"

"I will," he whispered, "I will in due time." He lowered the children to the steps beside his wife.

"Daddy's been to a fire, Mummie! Daddy's been to a fire!"

"What happened?" Marie asked.

Greg did not answer. He moved to the step below Marie and put her arms around him and his around her. Their faces were equal in height. His eyes glowed a soft blue as the setting sun winked in them. She caught the glitter.

"What happened?"

Greg pulled her gently to him and kissed her on the mouth, as if he were exploring her for the first time. The children gazed at them. Each touched the leg of each parent and then hugged them.

"Later," he said, "later. First I want to get a bath and eat."

After he showered, they sat for their meal.

Marie had prepared mashed potatoes, roast pork, garden peas, biscuits, and peach cobbler for dessert. Iced tea was the drink.

Greg always asked the blessing. He felt he was more qualified. It ran in the Butler family for men to ask the blessing in their homes. The men were in charge. Men knew God better than anyone else. They had closer contact with God. Man was God's right-hand person in all family matters.

Holding their hands Greg said, "Children, I want you to say the blessing tonight."

The children looked at each other and then at their parents.

"But Daddy, we never do that."

"I know," Greg said, "but say anything you want to."

"Okay, Daddy."

They bowed their heads and said, "Thank you, God, for Mummie and Daddy and bless them." Then they laughed. Greg and Marie smiled.

"Was that all right, Daddy?"

"That was all right."

Several times during the meal the children demanded, "Tell us about the fire, Daddy." Each time Greg answered, "Later. I have a long time to tell you about it. Don't worry. I will."

After the children were in bed, Greg and Marie sat at the kitchen table, drank tea and talked. The fluorescent light overhead cast a blue hue that highlighted Greg's face. It had lost the boyish fullness that followed him into manhood. His cheek bones rose strikingly above the hollows of his cheeks. His chin defined the dimple and his mouth was trim and relaxed as he told Marie about his mission, the fire, and the results.

At times, while he was talking, he closed his eyes and tried to concentrate, but found himself looking into his eyelids. He tried to stare through them. He looked into blackness scarred with red streaks and the blackness mixed with the red into a churning color, which looked like a storm, black and lead-grey, red and silver, turning in turbulence, a phantom imprinted inside his eyelids. It was as if a painter had flung a glob of black paint on a canvas, sprinkled it with reds and white and stirred it viciously.

He opened his eyes and reached across the table and held Marie's hands. Marie was captivated. She had always looked at him as her superior, as the force which controlled her life and she accepted that.

Now, she saw him as someone with all the weaknesses she had, and perhaps many more. It was a mysterious feeling that seemed to level Greg with her. A simple honesty about humanity. It was a humble feeling for the value of individual life.

"What's wrong, Greg?"

"It's not what's wrong, Marie, it's what's right."

He drew her hands toward him and bent and kissed them. Then he raised his head and as he said, "I'm going to give up the SWAT Team," something snapped inside him and a free motion began, like the balance wheel of a watch.

The free measuring of himself had begun. His spirit's movement was being regulated, smooth and constant, without a flicker of hesitation or fear.

"What are you going to do?"

"I don't know. But there's something out there I can do besides hunt a man to kill."

Cliff Barnhill

Cliff Barnhill walked stealthily toward the courthouse. His gangly frame curved as he walked with his head bent downward as if contemplating grave issues.

When he was a child, Cliff Barnhill, the only mortician in Ownes County, drew secret pleasure in manipulating the various extremities of animals. He soon realized that most creatures resisted the random moving and twisting of their body parts. Cats would scratch, dogs would snap, or at least yelp. Horses and cattle were too massive and would not yield to his whims.

At an early age he obtained an air rifle and managed to kill blue jays, mockingbirds and redbirds. Cliff liked the redbirds best, because they reminded him of blood.

Flying blood. He trapped rabbit and learned the rabbit punch from a local hunter and could dispatch a rabbit with one skillful blow behind the head. Sometimes he would beg for surplus raccoon, opossum, squirrel and muskrat from trappers.

In his search for pleasure, he prepared an altar beneath an oak, in the edge of the woods behind his house. Cliff named it his altar because he was an altar boy in church. He related the church altar to his altar.

He derived erotic pleasure as he moved legs and feet, nose and ears, twisting and contorting them into positions the animals could never have achieved in their living state. Cliff was transcendently ecstatic as he parted the feathers of the fowl and smelled the strange scent that came warmly from feather and flesh. He sank his nose into the fur of the rabbit, raccoon, opossum and muskrat and inhaled the exotic scent of animals passing from life into rigor mortis. He felt he was drawing into himself the secret force of the animal that enabled it to survive so well in nature.

In high school Cliff dated little. He resisted with much effort the desire to manipulate his date's body parts. Sometimes he failed to control himself and found he was in a frenzy manipulating her extremities. Relationships quickly ended.

After high school, he trained to be a mortician. This was his first step toward attaining his goal of opening his own funeral parlor.

Cliff wanted acceptance in the community and he felt it necessary to marry. He and his bride, Emily, settled in Hamlet, the Ownes County seat, joined all the right clubs and organizations, and borrowed money from the bank to open a mortuary.

Cliff decided to call the corpses he dealt with by their first names, never as the deceased. The people of Ownes County liked his approach, and with help from the sheriff he became mayor of Hamlet, a town of three hundred. Shortly afterward, he was elected county coroner.

He and the sheriff became friends but they did not drink together. Cliff took a glass of wine occasionally, and at dances he would have highballs.

The sheriff used Cliff as an expert witness and saw to it, through the judges, that he was well paid for his services. Cliff received little compensation as mayor but it gave him many business and political contacts for his plan to run for a county-wide office.

As Cliff entered the sheriff's office, the sheriff rose, limped to the door, and quietly closed it.

"How'ya doing, Sheriff?" Cliff asked, extending his hand. As they shook hands, the sheriff supported himself with his left hand on his desk.

"Pretty good, except for one thing."

"What's that, Sheriff?" Cliff's gimlet eyes flashed back and forth on the lawman.

"Remember that Burge man?"

"You talking about the one who burned to death in his house?"

"Yeah."

"What about him?"

"The DA wants us to hold an inquest. One with a jury."

"Why?" Cliff slid down into his seat. His body curved as if strung with an invisible bow string.

The sheriff placed both elbows on the desk and propped his chin in his hands, twisting his face. Cliff thought about body manipulation.

"People are talking all over the county. Some are saying we shot Burge and burned him up, which ain't true. You know the way Angra Kain is. He's trying to take over everything in the county. He's got control of the board of commissioners and now he wants my office. He's saying we didn't have to kill Burge, which we didn't kill him in the first place. He's saying that Burge was no criminal. The DA wants us to clear it up with an inquest. That will end all investigations. The matter will be laid to rest."

The sheriff appeared to be squeezing the words out of his mouth with his hands.

"Where is Burge?"

"His body is over in Kinston with Whitehead Funeral Home."

"Are we going to have to go over there?"

"No. We're gonna do it upstairs in the courtroom.

People around here never heard of a coroner's inquest. Don't know what one is. There's never been one that I know of in the county. We can just go on and have it and not tell anybody what's going on and everything will be all right."

"What about the jury?"

"Don't worry about the jury. I'll take care of it."

The sheriff lifted his head from his hands and clasped them in front of him. Cliff's eyes continued to glint off and on the sheriff.

"When you want to have the hearing?" The sheriff asked.

"How about Monday morning? That will give me time to bone up on the law and give you time to get the jury."

Hicks Wilson

Hicks Wilson ran a grocery store at the fork of Young's Crossroads. He sold a few canned goods, soft drinks, dried beans and peas, coffee, salt, salted pork, cigarettes, chewing tobacco, and snuff. He sold sugar mostly by the hundred pounds, a bootlegger's purchase.

Hicks supported the sheriff. A shrewd politician, he knew a sheriff was a difficult person to remove. For the last fifty years, sheriffs initially acquired office by appointment and remained in office until they died of natural causes or in auto crashes. Over the years many sheriffs had died of alcohol abuse in Ownes County. People came to believe that death by alcohol abuse was death by natural causes.

For Hicks, there was much gain expected in supporting the incumbent sheriff. They always needed whiskey for medicinal purposes, and Hicks could supply it. He also supplied sugar for many county bootleggers, with the sheriff's knowledge.

Ownes County sheriffs did not raid bootleggers. When the state Alcoholic Beverage Control officers came, somebody from the sheriff's office had to be with them on the raid. When the sheriff got word that an officer was on the way, he would always give warning to the bootleggers. The day before the raid he contacted them, saying, "Take your washing in, boys, take your washing in."

Several times the state undercover agents purchased non-tax-paid whiskey from Hicks and he had to appear in court. The sheriff, by talking to the judge, had the cases disposed of with a minor fine and costs.

For fifty dollars in hand Hicks could carry 90 percent of the black vote in his section of the county, which was 10 percent of the total vote.

"Got something I want'cha to do for me," the sheriff said.

Hicks, who was chewing tobacco, sat behind the counter on a stool, sweltering from the heat. Sheriff Tate had chosen mid-afternoon to visit because he knew there would be little business transacted then. Hicks rolled his bloodshot eyes, which looked like road maps, to the side and spit in a can beside the pot-bellied heater.

"What'cha need, Sheriff?"

The sheriff pulled a handkerchief from his pocket and mopped his brow. His face was red from the heat and Little Brown Jug.

"We need a rain to cool things off," he said as he looked about the store.

"I can't give you no rain, Sheriff," Hicks laughed, rolled his eyes and spit again, although he didn't need to. It was a habit he had developed to help him think, to deal with tense moments. He smelled something tense about the sheriff. He could tell when the sheriff was tense and serious.

"I got a jury I want you to sit on."

That was serious to Hicks. Negroes did not sit on the jury in Ownes County. In other counties maybe a few did. Very few.

"You know we don't sit on no jury, Sheriff." Hicks fixed his eyes on Tate. The blood vessels swelled across his eyes like lightning across the sky.

"You heard about Burge gittin' burned up, didn't you?"

"You talkin' 'bout that crazy fool living down the Catfish Lake Road?"

"Yeah."

"What about him?"

"The DA says we got to have a coroner's inquest. We got to have a coroner's inquest with a jury. We need six people. I want you to be one of them."

Hicks leaned over the counter, his jaws working the tobacco in a rhythmic frenzy. He spat viciously into the can.

"You want me to sit on that jury?"

"Yeah. All you got to do is do like I tell you. It'll be easy." The sheriff cleared his throat and lit a cigarette, then added, "Won't nobody even hear about it."

"Okay, that is, if you don't tell me too much," Hicks looked at him and smiled. Then he chuckled and added, "I'll do it, Sheriff, if you don't have too much to tell me."

"Come to the courthouse Monday morning at nine o'clock," the sheriff said as he peeled off two twenty-dollar bills and a ten.

"Election will be coming soon. You'll be needing this to carry voters to the polls. Don't worry, I won't have too much to tell you."

He passed the bills to Hicks and smiled.

Elsie Meadows

Elsie Meadows sat at the table on the screened-in porch. She wagged her tongue in the hollows left by her missing teeth. Flies buzzed and often pitched on the table. She brushed them away with the sweep of a fly swatter.

"Elsie, I got something I really need your help on," the sheriff said, laying his hat on the table between them. He mopped his face with his handkerchief. Sweat was seeping through his coat across his shoulders. Tate drew smoke from his cigarette into his lungs but did not expel it. He let it drift out of him through his natural breathing and it seeped out as if the words he was speaking were coming through a fire.

"What'cha got, Sheriff?"

"Remember Burge, that got burned up down the road?"

"You talkin' 'bout the Negro that defiled the church?"

Elsie Meadows was a preacher with her own church and preaching was the most serious thing in her life. All of her sermons opened with, "It is only by the blood of the Lamb. No other way for redemption!" She shouted and screamed, jumping off and on the square wood box she preached from. She mixed adultery, suicide, murder, rape, stealing and denying the Lord with the phrase, "It is only by the shedding of the blood of the Lamb that you can rid yourself of these sins!"

"I ain't no preacher," the sheriff added softly as he curled the rim of his hat with his fingers.

He thought about the annual hundred-dollar donation he made to her church. "But I know he was doing some things in the church he wat'nt suppose' to."

"Like that preaching naked, huh? Holding the people there with a gun. You know he had to be crazy, Sheriff."

"Yeah," Tate confirmed. He continued to curl his hat brim.

Flies soared over the table and Elsie drove them away with her fly swatter. "These flies are the worst this year I ever seen," she said as she swatted a fly. "What'cha got for me, Sheriff?" She asked as she brushed the dead fly off the table.

"The DA said we got to have a coroner's inquest and

find out the cause and means of Wardell's death."

"He got burned up, didn't he?"

"Yeah."

"There ain't nothing I can do 'bout that."

"I want you to sit on the jury."

"Me?" Elsie struck another fly and raked it off the table.

"You know we people don't sit on no jury in Ownes County."

"This ain't no regular jury. This is my jury and I can pick who I want. The county commissioners ain't got nothin' to do with who I pick. Hicks Wilson is going to sit. All we got to do is hear somebody testify about how he died and then sign a paper."

"You going to sit?"

"No, I'm going to be a witness. I'll be there to help you," He stood and pulled a roll of bills and counted off five twenties. "This will help you at homecoming." He grinned as he handed her the bills.

"I'll be there, Sheriff." She wagged her tongue and swatted another fly. "What time?"

"Nine o'clock Monday."

Travis and Odell

Travis and Odell Maides stood in Travis's front yard rolling their eyes like musket balls at the sheriff. They belonged to the Ku Klux Klan and didn't trust anyone. They worked with the sheriff in his elections, and the sheriff pretty much left them alone.

"I want to talk to you boys about sittin' on a jury."

The brothers rolled their eyes at each other, then back to the sheriff.

Travis was an expert black powder gunman. He knew the exact amount of powder for the distance of the target and could easily bring down a deer at one hundred fifty paces. Travis organized a black powder club, and the firing range was on his farm. He won a majority of the meets. The Maides brothers loved the old-fashioned way of loading guns. They felt connected directly to making power. The power to kill.

Odell's and Travis' eyes were as black as charcoal. Their skin was ruddy, their hair black and curly, their noses thick at the base, tapering quickly to a point. Travis was a half foot taller than Odell and was the leader. They thought alike. Travis did the thinking, and Odell agreed with him. What Travis said echoed in Odell's mind, and when he spoke he agreed with or repeated Travis.

Wardell Burge was familiar to them. They kept up with what they called radicals. He wasn't a problem to them because he was a bother to others of his race. The only other problem was his messing with the mail and that tickled them because they didn't agree with anything the government had anything to do with, including the mail. Taking all things into consideration, it was funny. A damn crazy coon taking over a coon church and preaching to them naked. That was funny, funny as hell. If he had been messing around a white church like that, a musket ball would have already found his head.

"You don't haf'ta come talk to us about that, Sheriff. You know we serve on the jury every time we're asked. We like to serve on the jury," Travis said.

Their eyes shot back and forth to each other and then to the sheriff.

"This is a different kinda' jury."

"Wha'cha mean, Sheriff?"

"This is going to be a coroner's jury to find out what the cause and means of Burge's death was."

Travis and Odell began laughing and slapping their thighs.

"It was a damn fire! Everybody knows it was a damn fire!"

Travis laughed the words between their laughter and leg slapping.

"I know," the sheriff said, "but Angra Kain is trying to stir some mess up about us startin' the fire and why come Burge didn't come out when the fire started. You know the way people think."

"You just want us to decide that it was a accident or something?"

"Yeah. That's right."

"See you at the polls, Sheriff," Travis said and rolled his eyes.

"See me at the courthouse on Monday morning at nine o'clock. That's when the inquest'll start."

Bunch Avery

Bunch Avery, a Marine retiree, polished his shoes every day, shaved, and kept a trim haircut. He believed in a strong military, and he believed military standards should be used in the public domain. Bunch was a strong believer in law and order. He believed in the free enterprise system and would go to almost any length to turn a profitable deal.

Bunch was in the insurance business: life, automobile and fire. He sold the sheriff a policy and became an insider with him. Tate gave Bunch tips on people to sell to throughout the county. Bunch could overlook the sheriff's consumption of alcohol when it conflicted with making a profitable deal. He came to look upon drinking as a necessary evil: evil that people did it, but necessary to transact business with them. Avery looked upon the sheriff as one of those necessary people.

"Avery," the sheriff said, pronouncing the word with a bump in it, "I need your help on somethin'."

They were sitting in the sheriff's office.

"What can I do for you, Sheriff?" Bunch crossed his legs and clasped his hands across his knee. The Marine Corps ring flashed from his left hand. His black hair, combed straight back, had the scent of Wildroot Cream Oil. He bounced his free leg up and down and smiled cautiously.

"I believe you believe in law and order, Bunch."

"I definitely do, Sheriff." Bunch continued to bounce his leg and smile.

"You remember about Burge don't you?"

"Yes."

"Have you heard any talk about it?"

Bunch's leg stopped bouncing and the smile disappeared.

They looked at each other. The sheriff held a steady gaze, like a plumb bob holds vertical.

"Yes, I have." Bunch paused and the sheriff waited.

"Well, what was it? What did you hear?" The sheriff asked.

"I've been hearing rumors that somebody shot him and set fire to his house. Of course they are just rumors."

"Rumors can start trouble. That's why we are going to

have a coroner's inquest with a jury to find out the cause and means of death."

The sheriff waited for Bunch to respond. He did not.

"Will you be willing to sit on the jury? I'm sure the evidence will show he set fire to the house and refused to come out." The sheriff unconsciously tapped with his knuckle in a slow, measured cadence on his desk.

"Yeah, Sheriff, I'll be glad to help you any way I can."

"I'll see to it you are foreman."

"When is it supposed to meet?"

"Nine o'clock Monday morning."

"Okay."

Dudley Howard

Dudley Howard was raking his yard. He was wearing short shorts, and sweat was running down his legs.

"You need to take a break," the sheriff said as he pulled into the yard.

Howard stopped raking and walked to the car. The sheriff smelled like the musky odor of alcohol mixed with sweat and unwashed body. Howard liked rank, wild smells. The smell of fear mixed with sweat and urine excited him most.

Dudley was recently charged with attempted rape, but the sheriff talked to the district attorney and the case was dismissed. When he was picking up slops for his hogs at Mrs. Thomas' house, he put his arms around her and attempted to kiss her. Mrs. Thomas insisted that she had had to use her elbows swiftly thrown to his midsection to repel him, because he was holding her from behind. The sheriff told the DA it was nothing but a prank, that they had received complaints from Mrs. Thomas before which didn't amount to anything.

"You looking for something?" Dudley asked, smiling as he approached the car. The sheriff made no effort to get out.

Dudley's smile was whimsical and friendly, yet people were skeptical of him.

He was a volunteer fireman and his pickup truck was equipped with a red light that flashed, and a siren.

"Yeah, you," the sheriff said and chuckled.

"Here I am," Dudley laughed through his smile.

The sheriff's arm hung out the window as if it had been broken. "It's hotter'n hell, ain't it?" He pulled his hat off and laid it on the seat. Sweat glistened on his puffed face.

"A little warm," Dudley placed both hands on the door on each side of the sheriff's arm. The sheriff said, "Got a little somethin' I want'cha to do for me."

"What'cha want me to do for ya', Sheriff?" Dudley's smile twisted into a quarter moon.

"Did you hear about Burge getting burned up down on the Catfish Lake Road?"

"Yea. I remember hearing." Dudley's mouth closed into a smile that went almost to his ears. His knee jerked up and down, forcing his body into rhythm.

"Well, the DA says we got to have a coroner's hearing to decide what he died of." The sheriff smiled with his mouth open. His broken and decayed, tobacco-stained teeth gleamed like sun-bleached rocks.

"Never heard of one."

"I want you to serve on it so you can find out what one is," the sheriff grinned.

"You gonna tell me what to do?"

"Sure am. You report to the courthouse Monday morning at nine o'clock."

For a moment they could not decide who would smile the longest as each stared into the other's face. The sheriff put his car into reverse, continued to smile at Dudley, and backed out of the yard.

Barnhill's Verdict

The courtroom was empty except for the apprehensive jurors who sat on the front row. They waited patiently until Sheriff Tate, the coroner, and the district attorney came out of the jury room. The eyes of the jurors, excepting the Maides brothers, followed the three men with trepidation. Travis and Odell drove at them with musket-ball eyes and smiled faintly. Howard smiled as if he were tired and weary.

The sheriff walked over to the jurors and said. "Okay, ya'll come on over to the jury box and have a seat."

Cliff Barnhill ascended to the judge's bench. Sheriff Tate handed Bibles to each juror. Cliff Barnhill swore them to make inquiry into the facts and bring in a verdict true and impartial according to the evidence.

"Ladies and gentlemen of the jury, we are assembled here today for an inquest to determine the cause and means of the death of one Wardell Burge. It is your duty under the law to take evidence and make a decision as to the cause and means of the death. Your decision will be true and impartial, based solely on the facts.

"If there are no questions," he waited briefly, looked at each juror and continued, "We shall take the evidence. Sheriff, call your witnesses."

The sheriff and Luke rose and placed their left hands on the Bible, raised their right hands, and faced the coroner, who swore them. "Take the stand, Sheriff."

Sheriff Tate rose, pulled his hat off and laid it on the table in front of the judge's bench. He limped to the stand and sat with his shoulders slumped forward. He held his hands clasped in his lap. Sweat popped out like blisters on his face. He stared toward the back of the courtroom through his thick, horn-rimmed glasses.

"Sheriff, were you at the death scene?" the coroner asked, fumbling through the papers on the bench.

Tate pondered momentarily and said, "Yeah. I was there."

"Tell the jury what happened."

Tate turned toward the jury, took a handkerchief from his pocket and mopped his face.

The jurors riveted on him and listened as he rehashed his version of the events leading up to the burning of

Wardell Burge.

Elsie Meadows twitched in her seat and wagged her tongue between her missing teeth. Her face writhed into a frown. Odell and Travis Maides rolled their eyes with disgust and hate. Bunch and Howard looked firmly at the sheriff and smiled.

"We went down there to get him."

The sheriff stopped and mopped his face and forehead. He looked at the sweat on his handkerchief and trembled when he continued.

"Then his mama come out and we got her to call for him to come out but he didn't."

He paused and continued, "Then something happened and I don't know what happened, but Burge shot from the window in the top middle of the house and smoke started coming out the window. That shot sounded different from the other ones. I don't know what happened but something did because smoke started boiling out the window on the top floor. We think the only thing that could have happened was for him to start it. Somebody had told us that he shucked and shelled corn up there for his pigs. He probably started the fire in them shucks. That's the only way we figure it could happen."

Sheriff Tate stared toward the back of the courtroom as if trying to read small print on the wall.

"Is there anything else, Sheriff?" The coroner prodded him.

The sheriff kept staring at the back of the courtroom. He was not sure if he was looking at the clock on the wall or the door beneath it.

"Is that all, Sheriff?"

"That's about it."

"Okay, Sheriff, you can step down."

Luke Hampton stood and said, "Mr. Coroner, I can testify but my testimony would be basically the same as the sheriff. I think you can let the record show that my testimony would corroborate the testimony of the sheriff. I tender myself to the court for any questions."

Barnhill turned to the jurors. "Do any of you have any questions for the district attorney or the sheriff?"

The jurors squirmed uneasily, ceased and remained quiet. The coroner stood, took some papers from the bench, and stepped down to the courtroom floor.

"You jurors come with me," he said as he went into the jury room.

The jurors followed. He closed the door and carried the papers to the table in the middle of the room.

"Okay, those of you who believe Burge started the fire and refused to come out when the fire got to going, sign this piece of paper right here and that will make it legal."

He spread the paper on the table and held it flat.

No one moved.

"All you got to do is sign it and it will be all right. It will be finished, done for, and you can get paid and go home."

"You know that's the only way it could 'uv been," Bunch said and stepped forward. As Cliff indicated the place, Bunch signed. Travis followed and then the rest.

"Now you can go down to the clerk's office and get paid," the coroner said.

Cliff Barnhill went to his private office in his mortuary and filled out the verdict of the coroner's jury. It read: after inquiring into the facts and circumstances of the death of the deceased from a view of the corpse and a consideration of all testimony to be procured, the jury finds as follows - that the deceased came to his death by suicidal means and was directly due to asphyxiation and burning, and that no criminal act or default was involved.

Angra's Plan

Angra Kain was pleased with the results of the audit of the clerk's office. Now he would turn his energies on the sheriff.

The sheriff had botched the Burge matter. People were talking about it all over the county. The fire and rescue squads spread the word. It wasn't what happened to Burge that mattered, as much as the bumbling, stumbling, drunken way the sheriff went about it.

Al Jackson had confided in Angra that he was planning on running for sheriff, and Angra had promised his support. Al was dead and out of the picture, but there was always someone out there who wanted to be sheriff.

If ever there was a time to strike, considering the

many rumors of the sheriff's drunkenness, some of them backed with witnesses, now was the time.

"Well, the sheriff is next," he said to Harold. He threw his legs over the end of his desk and laughed in a guttural growl. His voice hammered as if prying into the walls and ceiling, ripping off the paneling and Sheetrock.

"You can't do nothing with the sheriff. The sheriff is the most powerful man in the county. We can't make him do a thing," Sands, replied. He did not want a direct confrontation with the sheriff. Their working relationship was already bad enough, and he didn't want the sheriff campaigning against him in the next primary. Harold knew the sheriff could control the black vote.

Angra Kain slipped down in his chair, inserted his finger in his nostril and gently turned it, saying, "there is a proceeding to remove a sheriff from office if he is guilty of malfeasance of duty, whether intentional or not. If we can show that he ain't doing his job because of intoxication, then the judge will have to remove him. He's not entitled to a jury in that hearing. Just a judge. The judge would rule for us, I believe." Angra retracted his finger and took a drink of Old Taylor.

"Is that right?" Sands lifted his Old Taylor, mixed with 7-Up, and drank.

The two men often drank together at American Legion gatherings. Now that Harold was chairman of the board of commissioners they had become genuine drinking buddies.

He and Sands made board decisions in Angra's law office. They felt good making decisions for the county over a drink of bourbon.

"I'm getting all kinds of rumors about the sheriff's drinking," Angra spoke across his hands, which were folded over his stomach. "Are you hearing anything?"

"Yeah, I been hearing things," Sands replied.

"Do you know of anybody who has actually seen any of the things we've heard talked?"

Sands thought a minute, then responded, "I believe Hubert Perkins told me he was there when the sheriff was called to the house that burned down with that baby in it. Hubert is on the volunteer fire department, you know. He said the sheriff fell down and was too drunk to get up. That's one of the incidents." He took a sip from his glass.

"Knock'em Moore told me he was at the fairground when the sheriff tried to break up a fight and couldn't get out of his car. Have you heard anything about that?" Angra removed his feet from the desk and put a cigarette in his mouth.

"No, I ain't heard that but I heard something worse."

"What was that?" Angra struck a match. The fire spewed around the cigarette.

"About that time Albert Owens went to the courthouse to confess to murder and the sheriff couldn't even sign his name to the warrant. Albert hisself told that, I heard."

"Yeah. I heard something along that line. The hell of it is, Albert is off in prison. And there ain't nobody else I know that we can get to testify."

"Yeah. That's right."

"Anything else?"

"You remember last year when that Davis woman got killed? The one where her husband got drunk and beat her to death with a ax handle? Do you remember any talk about that?"

"I remember something about it."

"Well, I heard she had called the sheriff repeatedly that night and he never went nor did he send a deputy."

Angra leaned forward, "I believe there's enough stuff out there to get his ass! All we got to do is get our shit together and we can blow his ass out of the water. We'll shoot him with the big gun! We'll shoot him with what he is supposed to be—the law!"

Angra and Harold began to laugh. Their laughter joined and shook the room with a haughty shattering of silence. When the laughter subsided, Angra reached into his desk drawer, pulled out the bottle of Old Taylor and poured.

Scene

Sampson Gentry's barber shop. 2:00 P.M.

Barber shop, a counter, two sinks, two barber chairs along the right wall, a long bench half the length of the building, left.

Sounds of laughter, then Barber snaps apron in the air, places it around Farmer in first barber chair, begins snipping hair and talking current events with Logger and Salesman, seated on the bench.

Barber:	You boys hear about the break-in at the clerk's office?
Farmer:	Is that what they call it?
Logger:	I'd call it robbery.

Salesman: It smells like somethin' to me.

Farmer: Yeah, shit.

Barber: Now let's get this straight. I thought you had to have a gun or somethin' or take it from them by force. What I understand was somebody broke in and stole the stuff. Wasn't nobody in there when they took it.

(They laugh.)

Barber: Well, I guess you could say they used lead.

(They laugh.)

Salesman: The lead pencil, huh?

Barber: That ain't nothing new. They've been holding people up with lead just as long as people have been writing. That goes back a long time.

Salesman: I don't think Murray had anything to do with it.

Barber: He's driving a damn Cadillac, ain't he?

Salesman: Yea, but it's a used Cadillac. I sold him that car. It's a sixty-two. A damn good one, too!

(They laugh.)

Farmer: Reckon it's big enough to haul his money to the bank?

Logger: I don't know. Angra Kain said they were missing about sixty thousand. That's a lot to haul. Specially if it's in mixed bills.

Barber: Maybe it's time for him to get a new one.

Salesman: I really don't believe Murray knew anything about it.

Barber: You know the break-in happened right after they started the audit, don't you?

Logger: It did?

Barber: They had just started the audit and the next night was the break-in.

Farmer: Very convenient, huh?

Salesman: What did you say they got?

Logger: Angra Kain told me they got some cash money, they don't know how much, but they know there was two thousand dollars in one of the drawers. And Angra said they got some records, too. Bookkeeping records.

Salesman: How did they know how much money was in the drawer and what was the money doing in the drawer?

Logger: The auditor had counted it and it was supposed to go to the bank the next morning. Myrtle was supposed to put the cash and records in the vault overnight but somehow she accidently left them in the outer office. That's what Angra Kain said.

Barber: Did you hear how the burglar got in?

Farmer: No. How?

Barber: You know that little ledge around the courthouse? Well, I heard the sheriff said whoever went in walked that little ledge to the window and raised the window and went in and took what they wanted. The window wasn't locked, you know.

Logger: Very convenient.

Farmer: Convenient as hell.

Barber: Did the sheriff get any finger prints?

(They laugh.)

Logger: Smells like somethin' to me.

Barber: It might be like Anita was on Murray's wedding night.

Salesman: What you mean?

Barber: Don't you remember hearing about when Murray and Anita got married and on their wedding night she couldn't find his tallywhacker?

Salesman: Yeah. I remember hearing that.

Barber: That was serious business with Anita. That's what I heard. Heard she was hotter than a forty-ball tomcat. Up there in her head, that is.

(They laugh.)

Barber: Well, finding that money up there in the courthouse is kind'a like finding ole Murray's tallywhacker. It wasn't nowhere to be found.

Farmer: Tell you what. Time that crowd gets through with the courthouse there won't be nothing left but a brick.

Logger: What'cha mean?

Farmer: I mean when they steal all the money, they'll steal the damn courthouse and the only thing they'll leave will be one brick. To show their appreciation.

Salesman: Wonder which one was doing the most stealing?

Barber: I'd say the sheriff.

Salesman: Why?

Barber: Cause the sheriff sees double. That means he can steal twice as much as the rest.

(They laugh.)

Logger: Angra said he was going to get them out of there.

Farmer: You can't get crooks out of office. Ain't you heard about the old soldier? He don't die, he just fades away. It's like politicians and office holders, they don't die nor retire, they just steal away.

Barber: Stealing away. I like that. I believe you could say, according to the record we have of public officials, that stealing comes natural to them. Somehow or other they think they got to steal once they get in office. They think it's a obligation or something. They think it's a duty that comes with the office.

Logger: Yeah. Duty to steal until dead or kicked out.

Barber: Yeah. Can anybody in here remember or has anybody ever heard of a sheriff or clerk of court in this county ever to retire? No. Most of them died or got killed while in office or got kicked out of office because of natural causes. That is, if dying of alcoholism or getting killed while they were drunk is a natural cause. Or what don't get kicked out for stealing. If drinking and stealing are natural then dying while drunk or stealing would be natural causes.

Farmer: It's natural. It's a natural joke. Stealing and drinking in government is a natural joke.

Salesman: How did you say Angra was going to get the sheriff out?

Logger: Didn't say how. But he said there was a way. He said there was a way to bring him before a judge and if you can prove drunkenness to the point he can't do his job, then the judge can remove him.

Farmer: Has anybody seen him any other way?

Barber: You know what I heard? I heard they took

up more collection when Burge done his preaching than in the history of the church. They say it was the quietest sermon ever preached there. Religion was wide open. They say them old women were pulling up their dresses and dragging out them rolls of bills. Wasn't no singing and shouting and none of that hollering like, "You said it right, preacher! Tell'em about Daniel and the lion's den!" None of that. It was just straight, tight, bare-knuckle praying. And the sheriff just staggering around making little of it. Gettin' serious though, wonder what happened at that fire? Wonder if Burge really did set the fire?

Farmer: They busted his ass, that's what happened. But the truth won't never come out.

Barber: They shouldn't of done that.

Logger: The sheriff was between a rock and a hard place.

Farmer: They ought not burn up a crazy man. That's bad.

Logger: Let's get back to Angra and the sheriff.

Farmer: Knock'em Moore said the other day he saw the sheriff at the fairgrounds so drunk he couldn't stand up to stop a fight in front of the hoochie-coochie show. The American Legion boys had to take over.

Barber: Kent Jerkins was in here the other day and he said the sheriff was called to a fire out in Beaver Creek about two months ago and when he got there he was too drunk to get out of his car.

Salesman: Speaking of that, I heard a man went to the courthouse and tried to admit to a felony and the sheriff was too drunk to understand what he was saying. And you know what? I heard he went to lock somebody up, it was a man charged with larceny, I believe, and the sheriff locked himself up accidently and the prisoner walked out the door.

Logger: I reckon the sheriff felt at home. They tell me he sleeps off a lot of his drunks on the jail bunks.

Farmer: I've heard he does something else besides sleep down there.

Barber: You talkin' 'bout Myrtle?

Logger: You reckon he can still get it on?

Farmer: They say it's true.

Barber: I don't see how in the hell they can stand each other. But you know what they say. A stiff dick has no conscience. If I was either one of them, I'd rather take a killing than screw the other one.

Logger: The sheriff probably thinks he's screwing two at one time anyhow, that is if he can keep the bunk still long enough.

(They laugh.)

Salesman: I heard some time ago that he was called to Mrs. Davis's house up in the plantation and nobody from the department showed up and she wound up in the hospital because of a lick from a ax handle. It was her husband that done it.

Barber: I heard the same thing.

Farmer: You reckon they'll ever do anything about the kinda' people we got in office?

Salesman: They could if they wanted to.

Barber: Tell you what the problem is. The problem is when you got crooks in charge of everything they can't do anything. That's the trouble with everything. The crooks are in charge.

Luke's Decision

Luke Hampton sat stoically, staring at the television. Beverly sat beside him, waiting, in what seemed to her, a senseless world. She was learning the other side of love. Now, she knew the meaning of the phrase, "until death do us part." She was forever at his side during his sickness, responding to his every need. Regretfully, she knew that she could not respond to that which he wanted most-more quality life and the deference of the cancer.

After the coroner's inquest, Dr. Parker told Luke, "It's spreading fast. Faster than any I have ever treated. You have a very short time."

Luke didn't want anybody to touch him. It wasn't that he thought anybody would contaminate him or he them. He was alone, and nobody could erase that. That's the way it had to be. Out of all the touching, the treating, the caring, there was nothing left except him, staring out of himself into the abyss, waiting for the summon. It was he alone who had to give up the ghost and depart to where no traveler had returned. He liked Shakespeare. He hit with the truth.

Dr. Parker had sat facing Luke with his hand on Luke's knee as he talked. Luke had moved his knee enough so Dr. Parker would move his hand, but not enough to show he was shuffling it off.

"We could send you to Duke. They have a new procedure that's proved helpful."

Dr. Parker paused. His eyes wandered over Luke's face. He wasn't sure Luke had heard him.

"I said they have a new procedure at Duke that might prolong your life," he said. He read the rejection on Luke's face.

"Okay then, we better start your chemotherapy."

After five treatments Luke's weight loss was significant. His cherubic face sunk around the contours of cheek and jaw. His eyes, once cheerful, now glowed dimly as if through smoke. Most of his hair had fallen out, leaving nothing but a thin rim running the base of his skull, even with the top of his ears. It was as if a terrible drought had stricken a farmer's field and left it bare with windblown sand, leaving nothing but a rim of trees around its border.

Luke was watching a talk show. The host ran down the middle aisle and forced himself between the rows of seats and thrust his microphone toward a police officer's mouth-so close the officer recoiled.

"I'll ask you the same question! Do you believe a police officer should have the right to shoot a person who is suspected of having committed a felony, when the suspect flees, after the officer orders him to stop?"

That was the only thing Luke heard of the program. He had been staring at it for fifteen minutes, unaware of his surroundings. He blinked his eyes and looked toward the door.

The nausea was bothering him. It was as if an alien creature had moved into his being, pushed him aside and taken over his life. If it took over, then he would become a sideline watcher to a dissipater of life. It was as if life were sick of itself and that was worse than pain. Pain was stark. You fight pain or totally give in, relinquishing to the immensity of it. Nausea was like being sick of yourself, and when you are sick of yourself, there is nothing left except naked shame.

"Mr. Hampton, you're next," the technician said poking her head out the door of the treatment room.

Luke rose and moved to the aisle near him, then turned and headed toward the door.

"This way, Mr. Hampton!" the technician called.

"Where are you going?" Beverly called behind him.

"Home," Luke said as he walked out the door.

Angra's Charges

Cliff Barnhill read the pleadings. The words jumped off the pages like vipers attacking and sinking their poisonous fangs into the flesh of his ally, Sheriff Tate. Cliff knew the law demanded that the coroner serve papers on the sheriff in lawsuits against him.

He read and re-read the petition, folded it and put it in his coat pocket.

These were charges. That's all they were. He felt the sheriff would be exonerated. They were allegations brought on by Angra Kain to remove the sheriff and put in his own man. If Angra kept on, he would control the entire county. Cliff decided the charges were false, that people would have to lie to prove the things alleged. He did not believe that many people would lie on the witness stand. Cliff knew the sheriff well, and he had never seen him when he could say he was drunk. In his dealings with him the sheriff may have had the smell of whiskey occasionally on his breath, but he was not drunk.

It was five-thirty on the last day of July. The sheriff would be alone in his office. Now was the time to serve him. He rose, left his office with long strides and curved his body toward the courthouse.

The sheriff was sitting behind his desk smoking a cigarette. He did not move when Cliff sat. His hands cupped together and his chin rested on his thumbs. The smoke curled out of his hand in a thin coil, drifted up and disintegrated in a violet veil about his face.

"Damn, it's hot in here." Tate drew from his cigarette and wiped his brow.

He had suspicions why Cliff was there. Rumors had been grinding out in bits and pieces about his drinking, and he heard Angra was behind it. Sheriff Tate had been trying to wean himself from the bottle but it wasn't working very well. The diseases were coming at him from all sides: Angra Kain; Myrtle, now on the verge of death; his prize deputy shot to death; all they had to do was slam the coffin lid in Luke's face; that Burge thing; and Murray, hounded into not running for re-election.

What life he had left was hanging on the bare threads of despair and hope. He was beginning to believe the diseases were undefeatable.

Weren't the diseases necessary? His was. He could not survive without the disease. The sheriff could not hold the burden of all the other diseases without a cushion. Survival was hell for the individual. Survival for society was hell many times doubled and diseases worked like maggots of destruction in the bowels of society.

"What'cha got, Cliff?"

"Got to do something I don't want to do, Sheriff." Cliff uncrossed his legs and shuffled his body around in his chair.

A silence quietly bonded them. Previously, they had operated together for a common reason, to keep power for themselves and survive economic and social demands. Now, as they looked at each other, they knew they were bonded by a common cause: to keep the sheriff in office.

"Gimme the papers."

Cliff handed him the papers and moved uneasily in the chair.

"I'll accept," the sheriff said. He scrawled his signature on the papers. "I'm gonna get myself admitted to Walter B. Jones Alcoholic Rehabilitation Center. They say that's the best one around here. I'm gonna get ready for the son'bitches."

He put his hat on and cupped his hands beneath his chin and leaned on them. He read the allegation. "The sheriff of Ownes County, Earl Tate, has attempted and continues to attempt to perform the duties of sheriff while in a state of intoxication."

Cliff twisted in his chair and said, "Sheriff, I'll testify for you. I don't know of any time I've seen you in the condition they describe in the petition."

"I'd appreciate that." The sheriff pushed the papers back to Cliff, rose, and limped to the stairs leading down to the jail.

"I'm gonna try to get in tomorra'," he said as he braced against the wall and made his way with painstaking care down the steps.

Tate's Trial

During Sheriff Tate's sixty-day treatment at the Walter B. Jones Rehabilitation Center, Angra Kain prepared his case against him. He talked to the fireman who were at the scene of the Burge burning. All of them agreed to testify that the sheriff was intoxicated at the fire. He held meetings with everyone involving the incidents he and Harold Sands had discussed. Each said they had seen Tate on numerous occasions intoxicated while he was trying to perform his duties. They all agreed to testify for Angra. Even a former deputy agreed to testify. There was no question in Angra's mind that he had sufficient evidence to remove the sheriff for malfeasance. He knew, because he was suing a public official, he must have more than the greater weight of evidence, he must have an overwhelming preponderance of evidence. He thought he had it.

Tate returned from the Walter B. Jones Rehabilitation Center sober and pallid. It was the first time he had been completely sober in ten years. He realized how much the world had changed. He appeared different. His limp was not as pronounced and things were not in a constant blur. He was ready for trial. He was ready to fight Angra Kain.

Tate hired Strom Newman, a young aggressive attorney from New Berne. Newman was distant kin to the sheriff. He believed in defending his blood. Newman was intelligent, perceptive and an expert on cross examination. He knew the judges who were close friends of the sheriff.

Many superior court judges who had held court in Ownes County, including Judge Odom, assigned to conduct the inquiry, had taken a drink with the sheriff. Tate had at times furnished some of them with quality bootleg whiskey and local wine.

"It's too good to throw out. Too wasteful," Judge Moore had said as he sniffed and touched the jar to his lips. "I'll take this one."

The board of commissioners hired a special prosecutor from Kinston to assist Angra Kain with the prosecution.

Judge Jiles Odom was a college roommate with Judge Moore, who lived in Hobbs County. Odom was a guest at the home of Judge Moore while he tried the case against the sheriff.

When the trial began, Judge Odom sat sternly and listened intently as Kain presented the witnesses to factually prove the allegations of intoxication against Sheriff Tate. His face twisted occasionally as if he were being forced to take small doses of arsenic. Newman cross-examined the witnesses about whether they had at some time taken a drink with the sheriff. He examined their capability to determine intoxication and eliminated the use of the word, drunk, from their testimony. Newman questioned them as to their political preference in the upcoming sheriff's race. He made the trial a political issue.

The first four witnesses for the sheriff were bootleggers who swore they had never seen the sheriff in a drunken state. The next two witnesses were superior court judges who testified they often held court in Ownes County, and dealt with the sheriff in his office and in open court. They had never smelled whiskey on his breath nor seen him when they considered him to be intoxicated. The sheriff of Onslow County testified likewise.

Luke Hampton measured each step as he approached the witness stand. He fingered the arm rest, like a blind man, as he helped himself into the chair. His voice was thin and it rasped with a tin-like quality as he spoke. He did not look at Strom Newman nor Angra Kain when they questioned him. The top of his head shone like a bone in the sun. He looked at the back of the courtroom as he testified that occasionally he had taken a drink with the sheriff but never saw Tate when he thought Tate was drunk. Luke testified that in his opinion he had never seen Tate drunk while performing his duty.

He felt, as he talked, he was testifying for the ghost of justice, which was always out of man's reach. The sheriff was sober wasn't he? The hearing had served its purpose. The people had a sober sheriff. Surely after this he would stay sober.

Dimly he saw justice emerge as a battle, with the law as weapons, between opposite ends of society. It was simply a fight for power. Fueled by the will for power, whichever side won flew the banner for justice. He trembled and wavered as he hobbled back to his seat.

The sheriff took the stand and underwent four hours of grueling cross examination. He admitted taking a drink before evening meals and taking social drinks with many of the men who testified against him. He denied ever being unable to perform his duties because of intoxication. He said his limp and the crook of his neck was due to ancient injuries. He did not vary his testimony.

As the sheriff's witnesses testified, Judge Odom relaxed as if he had taken a tranquilizer and had been relieved from secret pain.

After the evidence was taken, the judge, his face filled with vitality, was eager to express himself. He leaned over the bench, adjusted his robe, tilted his glasses on the bridge of his nose, and peered across them. He laid his hands palms down on the bench, pursed his lips and spoke.

"This has been an unmitigated, unparalleled political attack, the most underhanded and insidious denouncement of a public official that I have ever witnessed. It is a display of insensitivity, attacking a respected and honorable public official, Sheriff Tate, of Ownes County.

"If there are any apologies they should be from those who instigated this outrageous inquiry. It is obvious that this is a political maneuver to either remove the sheriff or cause him public embarrassment that would harm him in his re-election bid. And I charge those of you who are responsible for this inquiry, if you have any political linen to wash, wash it at the polls!"

He paused, pursed his lips again, leaned further over the bench and added, "I hereby deny the allegations in the petition! Court dismissed!"

The sheriff rose and limped to the bench.

"Thank you, Judge," he said and offered his hand.

It was strange to the sheriff that he didn't hate Angra Kain. He saw him as a disease roaming free in society, making its way through power. All he wanted was to be sheriff, have a good income and be respected. To take a drink once in awhile so the diseases would leave him alone. That was all he wanted.

It was late on a Friday when the trial ended. After rounds of congratulations to the sheriff, the courthouse cleared. Tate invited Murray to his office.

"One thing about it," he said, "they proved Little Brown Jug won't make you drunk." He chuckled as he reached in his desk drawer, pulled out a fifth, opened it and took a swallow.

Things were going too fast for him again. He needed to slow them down. Whiskey did that for him. After he took the first two big drinks, it seemed to speed things up, but when he stayed with as much as he could carry, things slowed as if he were outside all the activity swirling around him.

He could once again sit back or walk slowly or drive carefully and watch the diseases run their courses. He saw many of them out there. Assaults, illegal liquor sales, murder, incest, rape, larceny, adultery.

Myrtle was dying. He had always cared for the old thing. They made good partners. He decided to go to the hospital to see her.

The Sheriff's Goodbye

Myrtle lay motionless. The sheriff sat next to her smoking a cigarette. Overhead, the neon lights buzzed like moth wings. He pulled on his cigarette and blew the smoke lazily out of his mouth, watching it break into a grey mist which hung listlessly above his head.

"No," she said, "Don't worry about smoking. It's not my lungs. It's my blood. My lungs are good. I've never had a problem with my breathing."

Myrtle believed in the clean life. No alcohol or smoking. No red meat in her diet. She did not teach her young women to smoke nor did she teach against it. She was pleased, though, that none of them smoked. Her church taught against smoking and this was to her advantage. Most of the time they had not begun smoking and under her tutelage they refrained.

The sheriff looked at the strange aura on her face but he refused to comprehend it. She was not smiling, but she looked as if there was a smile beneath the exterior of her face. It had a fixed mood that belied deep secret pleasures that she revealed only to herself and her young friends. It was the knowledge of secretly sharing pleasure. Myrtle always wore that mood, but her young women did not look at the mood for a source of pleasure. It was the erotic pleasure and physical intimacy she brought with her kisses, her tongue, and her roving hands and fingers that they craved.

Now her eyes were a dull bronze. Her skin was a washed grey. Beneath the skin, beige blotches floated, as if they were freckles suspended in the flesh itself, and had the power of mobility, as leaves under water. Her frog-like lips rolled out into a voluptuous puckering as she spoke.

"They don't know what it is. I'm losing the battle quickly." Myrtle's lips rolled out, then settled back firmly.

The sheriff thumped the ashes off his cigarette without looking. Myrtle's hair was in a perm that rolled like a halo around her face. Her eyelids drooped, hanging just above the pupils. The intensity of her life force glimmered faintly.

"You reckon there ain't nothing they can do for you

at the Duke Cancer Center?"

Myrtle's chest moved stintingly. Her lips rolled out and hissed the words, "The doctors say not. They've talked to Duke."

Her lips rolled back, half-parted. Myrtle's face was grim and fixed with determination, yet her spirit was waiting for the time to steal away and abandon its vessel.

She felt cheated. A woman ripe with passion and eager to share it, snared by the tentacles of an alien force sapping her lifeblood. Myrtle's regrets were not about how she had lived her life. She resented the irrevocable short circuiting of the passion and pleasure of her life. The disease that was killing her was like a mysterious magnet drawing her strength, her mind, her desire, her interest, from the very force of her blood and the marrow of her bones.

Nothing about her moved. The sheriff rose, went to her bedside and kissed her lips. There was no response.

"Goodbye, Myrtle." He straightened up, put on his hat, and limped out the door.

Tate's Fog

Sheriff Tate liked October. It was the time of harvest, to make fruitful the year's labor. This October was different. Luke had died of brain cancer, Myrtle had wasted away and died of a strange blood disease, Mrs. Burge had died of another heart attack in August and of coarse Al Jackson.

This October, frost came late and fog lingered across the fields and roads in a thin, grey veil. The mornings were cool and hunters were preparing their guns for the season.

The sheriff was content that he had appointed Alvin Hill, his black part-time deputy, who was a bootlegger, to take Al Jackson's place. Now Alvin would be his only full-time deputy.

Sugar, as Alvin was affectionately called, sold tax-paid whiskey, after the ABC stores closed, to many people in Hamlet. Most were white because they could afford his prices. As the word spread, he had customers from beyond the county line.

He soon learned it would be one of his duties to keep a supply of Little Brown Jug at the sheriff's disposal. Sugar kept several bottles available in the sheriff's desk drawer.

He got off work at nine in the evenings, unless a situation was pressing. From nine at night to early morning he sold tax-paid whiskey.

Sugar's operation was protected by the law. He slyly informed blacks and poor whites that he was the law. He was his own protection. Sugar was also physically formidable. He was tall and his body was muscled from many years of finishing cement and driving pipe for water wells. He didn't mind slapping his own kind to put them in line. Firm words worked on the whites.

The Alcoholic Beverage Control officers failed to make undercover purchases. Sugar refused to sell to strangers and that further protected his operation.

Sugar purchased a small piece of land and built a house for his wife and four children. He kept a jackass and a pair of geese in his backyard hog pen. He barbecued pigs in his back yard and sold the barbecue to the folks who worked in the courthouse and county offices, and shipped some north each week.

Now, there were hardly any violations of the law to deal with. Everything was growing dull. Even the passing of time. As the sheriff moved into this period of tranquility, his drinking increased.

Before this calm, it was as if a hive of hornets had gone berserk, attacking everything in sight. In his mind the whole world had been shrieking and hollering as if at Halloween, and suddenly it was out of breath, exhausted, and there was nothing left but the hideous laughter of the clowns and entertainers.

As his intake of alcohol increased, the sheriff realized he was constantly having double vision. This didn't bother him. He learned to compensate for the double vision by reducing his speed to thirty miles per hour when he drove. Even after reducing his speed he had several fender benders that Bunch settled without an investigation.

When everything became blurred, he decided to do something. He decided he must have a personal driver.

Sugar Hill was delighted to consider taking on another duty. He knew the sheriff drank, and, maybe at times, a little too much. But he would defend with his life the right of the sheriff to do it. He knew Angra Kain was still after the sheriff but the sheriff had made him chief deputy and, he reasoned, that was more than any other colored man had ever achieved in Ownes County. That was something to consider. If they were out to get the sheriff, they were out to get him, and that was the only way you could look at it, he decided.

The sheriff lived eight miles from Hamlet and drove back and forth each day until he decided he must have a driver. Tate devised a new schedule. Sugar was to go to the office at seven-thirty in the morning and wait for the sheriff to call. Then Sugar would go pick him up.

Sugar would serve papers during the day and keep a lookout until five o'clock. Unless the sheriff needed him, he would go home and wait for the sheriff to call to take him home.

There was one exception. If the sheriff did not call in the morning it meant he was going to drive. This happened about once a week, on Monday.

With Sugar driving, the sheriff would stare out the window into the motion. The pine, cypress, gum and oak trees, and the houses and barns, sped by in a whirlwind. Dark and pale greens rushed together silently, churning and mixing into a fast spin. The buildings moved as if sliding. Time and motion were mixing things into a helpless blend. He was apart from it all, anchored on a vortex of stillness with nothing about him alive except his blurring eyes.

Everything in the past had been coming apart. Now everything outside him was coming at him in a crazy motion, moving in a vicious whirlwind of twirling, hurling, light, crashing into matter, breaking everything up into itself. Everything mixed into a blur, and the blur was all there was.

There was nothing out there but motion and mixing and nothing had itself unto itself because of the motion.

He sat in his cocoon, watching the chaotic blur.

The diseases, I have finally escaped them, he mused, as the road twisted backward swiftly and silently, as if sucked violently into a maelstrom. The forest moved slowly in one massive heap along the horizon, as if it were a sliding mountain pinned to the roadside with a down gear. Distance moved slowly and nearness moved swiftly.

The word, disease, flew like a swallow through his mind and vanished. Quickly, he left his mind to the solitude of watching motion.

Once he asked, "Sugar, what do you want to be when you grow up?"

"When I grow up?" Sugar cackled, mouth stripping open to reveal a vast chasm of white teeth, "I want to be just like I am," he said, and laughed.

"Me too," the sheriff said, "I've always wanted to be just like I am." He smiled and gazed down the road which seemed to be running into the car. It was motion and matter mixing before him in frightful proportions.

He reached in the glove compartment, pulled out a bottle and took a drink, not taking his eyes off the road.

In early November, Sugar waited anxiously to hear from the sheriff. The morning had been extremely foggy and there were patches still lingering in low places. It was nine-thirty and he would have called by then. He was rarely late. Sugar should have heard from the sheriff.

Sugar decided to wait and check the mail. If he hadn't heard by then, he would call.

While he was going through the mail the phone rang.

"Sheriff's office," Sugar answered.

"There's been a terrible accident down at Oliver's Crossroads! The sheriff's involved! I've just called the rescue!" A frantic voice blared.

Sugar did not hesitate. He was in his cruiser speeding ninety miles an hour before he could even think and when he did, he asked himself, "Wonder what happened?"

They decided later that the cause of the accident was smoke from a woods fire. A farmer had burned a field the evening before and when night fell, the wind came up and roused smoldering debris which erupted into flames. The fire ate into the woods and the smoke from it mixed with the night fog. By morning, visibility in the area was minimal.

A truck hauling a load of sheet metal had entered the smoke and fog too quickly and rammed the rear end of a car which was making its way slowly through the smoke. The car was crushed in the rear and sitting at an angle. Tate was unaware of the smoke and fog until he was in it and then it was too late to keep his cruiser from collision. The hood of his cruiser slipped beneath a piece of sheet metal extending from the truck body.

Sugar approached with his bubble blinking. A man directing traffic had stopped a line of cars. By the time Sugar got out of his car the rescue squad arrived.

The man directing traffic ran up to the rescue squad ambulance and yelled, "Better go in there quick as you can!"

He pointed to the smoke and fog.

"Let's get in there! I want to get the sheriff out!" Sugar bellowed, waving at the driver of the rescue squad ambulance.

"Okay. Easy." Sugar directed as the ambulance moved slowly toward the sheriff's vehicle.

Sugar went to the driver's side of the car.

The piece of sheet metal had penetrated the windshield at a height just above the sheriff's shoulders.

The sheriff's chin appeared to sit atop the sheet metal. His fatuous face was fixed with the awful insensitivity of non-awareness. His hands still gripped the steering wheel.

"What happened, Sugar?" He turned his head, grinning, with his mouth agape, showing his tobacco-stained teeth, adding, "We're gonna beat the hell out'a them in the election, ain't we Sugar?" He chuckled.

APPENDIX A

NCGS 15-48 DECLARED UNCONSTITUTIONAL

An analysis of NCGS 15-48 by the United States District Court reveals the barbaric mentality of the law. It is, in effect, a death warrant.

Gerald W. AUTRY, on his own behalf and on behalf of all others similarly situated, Plaintiff,

v.

Burley B. MITCHELL, Jr., District Attorney for the Tenth Judicial District, on behalf of himself and all others similarly situated, Defendant.

No. 75-0344-CRT-5.

United States District Court,
E. D. North Carolina,
Raleigh Division.

Oct. 14, 1976.

On a challenge to the constitutionality of the North Carolina outlawry statute, a Three-Judge Court, Craven, Circuit Judge, held that the statute was procedurally deficient under the due process clause of the Fourteenth Amendment, and was also capricious and irrational in violation of the equal protection clause of the Fourteenth Amendment.

Declaratory judgment granted; injunctive relief denied.

1. Constitutional Law 42.1(3)

One declared an outlaw, or his administrator, was not obliged to wait until he had been wounded or killed in order to obtain standing to bring suit challenging constitutionality of North Carolina outlawry statute. G.S.N.C. 15-48; Fed.Rules Civ.Proc. rule 23, 28 U.S.C.A.

2. Arrest 59
Constitutional Law 258(3)

North Carolina outlawry statute is procedurally deficient, under due process clause of Fourteenth Amendment, in various respects. G.S.N.C. 15-48; U.S.C.A. Const. Amends. 8,14.

3. Constitutional Law 211(2)

Whenever statutory classification affects fundamental rights, it will encounter equal protection difficulties unless justified by compelling governmental interest. U.S.C.A. Const. Amend. 14.

4. Constitutional Law 213.1(2)

Traditional equal protection test is invidious discrimination, sometimes denominated the "rational basis" test. U.S.C.A. Const. Amend. 14.

5. Constitutional Law 250.1(2)

North Carolina outlawry statute insofar as treating same offenders differently in that some accused murderers who failed to surrender were outlawed and many others were not was capricious and irrational and violative of equal protection clause, and statute was irrational in other respects as well. G.S.N.C. 15-48; U.S.C.A. Const. Amend. 14.

Norman B. Smith, Smith, Patterson, Follin, Curtis & James, Greensboro, N.C. for plaintiff.

Rufus L. Edmisten, Atty. Gen., Joan H. Byers, and Jack Cozort, Associate Attys, North Carolina Dept. of Justice, Raleigh, N.C., for defendant.

Before CRAVEN, Circuit Judge, LARKINS, Chief District Judge, and DUPREE, District Judge.

MEMORANDUM OF DECISION

CRAVEN, Circuit Judge:

I.

On August 14, 1974, Gerald W. Autry was a fugitive from justice charged with first degree rape, felonious assault, robbery with a dangerous weapon, and assault and battery. Pursuant to N.C.G.S. 15-48, set out fully in the margin,[1] Autry was declared an outlaw. He turned himself in to Wake County law enforcement officers the same day and thereafter brought this suit to declare the outlawry statute unconstitutional and to enjoin its future enforcement. He asked that the action be certified as a class action and that plaintiff's class be constituted of all persons who have been declared outlaws or who may in the future be declared outlaws; he further sought that defendant's class be held to constitute all district attorneys of the State of North Carolina and other officers and persons who have applied, or in the future may apply, for the issuance of outlawry proclamations to the statute.

In a memorandum opinion and order entered February 4, 1976, Chief Judge Larkins held that Mr. Autry met the requirements of Rule 23, Federal Rules of Civil Procedure, and is well able to fairly and adequately protect the interests of the plaintiff class. Since he was not proceeding pro se but was represented by counsel, we agree, and, for the reasons stated by Judge Larkins, we certify the class sought by the

---

[1] The statute reads as follows:
In all cases where any justice or judge of the General Court of Justice shall, on written affidavit, filed and retained by such justice or judge, receive information that a felony has been committed by any person, and that such person flees from justice, conceals himself and evades arrest and service of the usual process of law, the justice or judge is hereby empowered and required to issue proclamation against him reciting his name, if known, and thereby requiring him forthwith to surrender himself; and also empowering and requiring the sheriff of any county in the State in which such fugitive shall be to take such power with him as he shall think fit and necessary for the going in search and pursuit of, and effectually apprehending, such fugitive from justice, which proclamation shall be published at the door of the courthouse of any county in which such fugitive is supposed to lurk or conceal himself, and at such other places as the justice or judge shall direct; and if any person against whom proclamation has been thus issued continues to stay out, lurks and conceals himself, and does not immediately surrender himself, any citizen of the State may capture, arrest, and bring him to justice, and in case of flight or resistance by him, after being called on and warned to surrender, may slay him without accusation of any crime. (1866, c.62; 1868-9, c.178, subch. 1, s.8; Code s.1131; Rev. s.3183; C.S., S.4549; 1969, c.44, s.30; 1971, c.1141, s.9.)

plaintiff and hereinafter view the action as one brought for the benefit of all persons who have been outlawed or who may in the future be outlawed pursuant to N.C.G.S. 15-48.

Judge Larkins did not undertake to decide whether to grant plaintiff's prayer to join as parties defendant all district attorneys and others who have sought to utilize the statute or who may in the future do so. We think the reasons he advanced for certifying plaintiff's class apply with equal force to certification of the requested class of defendants. The defendant Burley B. Mitchell, Jr., is himself an experienced and able prosecutor well versed in both the procedural and substantive aspects of the criminal laws of North Carolina. We think he knows as well as any prosecutor would know the utility and value of the challenged statute and is well able to define its proper scope and defend its constitutionality. Moreover, it should be noted that Mr. Mitchell is capably represented by competent staff members of the office of the Attorney General of North Carolina, who is himself capable of representing the interests of the public and the prosecuting attorneys within the state. Accordingly, we certify defendant's class to contain all district attorneys and other officers and persons who have applied, or in the future may apply, for the issuance of outlawry proclamations pursuant to N.C.G.S. 15-48. We find the facts to be as alleged in paragraph five of the complaint with respect to the establishment of this class.

[1] Mr. Mitchell and the members of his class initially defend on the ground that Autry and others who may have been outlawed, or who may be outlawed in the future, lack standing, and that there is no justiciable controversy. This question was previously presented to Chief Judge Larkins by way of motion for summary judgment and was denied by him. We adopt his memorandum opinion and order, entered February 4, 1976, as our own, and join and concur with Judge Larkins in holding that the plaintiff and others similarly situated, heretofore or hereafter, have a personal stake in the outcome of the controversy sufficient to assure that the dispute will be presented, as it has been, in an adversary context. We agree with Judge Larkins that one who has been declared an outlaw (or his administrator) need not wait until he has been wounded or killed in order to obtain standing to bring a suit challenging the validity of the statute.

II

[2] Autry and the members of his class impugn the constitutionality of N.C.G.S. 15-48 on the grounds that the statute denies procedural due process and equal protection of the laws to those persons declared to be outlaws in violation of the Fourteenth Amendment of the United States Constitution. We agree, and hold the statute unconstitutional. We put to one side Autry's attack upon the statute as incompatible with the Eighth Amendment prohibition of cruel and unusual punishment.[2] N.C.G.S. 15-48 means this:

The judges of North Carolina *shall* outlaw any person charged by affidavit

[2] If the statute is viewed as a penal one, we would have little difficulty in concluding that authorizing citizens to slay an outlawed person with impunity is so disproportionate to the underlying status of accused felon as to be cruel in its excessiveness and unusual in its character and inconsistent with evolving standards of decency that mark the progress of a maturing society. Trop v. Dulles, 356 U.S. 86, 101, 102, 78 S.CT. 590, 2 L.Ed.2d 630 (1958).

with a felony if it appears in the affidavit that the accused person evades arrest, by having fled or concealed himself, and will not submit to service of process. Anyone may file such an affidavit. The judge is without discretion: the statute does not authorize him to consider whether or not the affidavit is true, or whether the felon is dangerous to others, or whether such an extreme measure is wholly inappropriate and unnecessary. Indeed, as the statute is drawn the judge does not act as a judge but acts ministerially and is *required* to issue the proclamation upon presentation of a facially sufficient affidavit. The effect of the proclamation is to license the public to kill the accused felon if he runs after being called on to surrender.

A.

We hold the statute procedurally deficient under the Due Process Clause of the Fourteenth Amendment in these respects:

(a) It is not required that an impartial judicial officer determine probable cause, *i.e.*, that a felony has been committed and that the person proposed to be outlawed probably committed it.

(b) Alternatively, it is not required that an arrest warrant have been issued or an indictment returned by a grand jury.

(c) It is not required that an arrest warrant or other process have been served, or an attempt made to serve it, and a return made that the accused is not to be found within the county.

(d) There is no provision for notice and opportunity to be heard. The State's argument that a fleeing felon does not wish to be heard and would not avail himself of the opportunity is fallacious. It is commonplace for those who deny the validity of judicial process to appear specially by legal representative and to move to quash summons and process. If there were simply notice to show cause, the family of an accused felon might hire counsel to quash the proclamation for the purpose of diminishing the risk of death. But the proclamation is issued ex parte, without notice to anyone, and without provision for a hearing or for any lapse of time within which to conduct it.

B.

The North Carolina outlawry statute, as implemented, recognizes three classes of accused felons: (1) a large group who presumably are arrested or surrender soon after indictment or accusation; (2) hundreds and perhaps thousands per annum who are not quickly arrested and who do not surrender but are nevertheless *not* outlawed; and (3) perhaps one or two, and certainly no more than a half dozen, who are outlawed annually. Counsel have furnished us a partial list of North Carolina's 20th century outlaws. According to that compilation, we know only of a total of 20 outlaws beginning in 1943 and running through 1975. The only consistent difference we can discern between the outlaws and the thousands of fleeing accused felons who have *not* been outlawed is that with respect to the former someone filed an affidavit resulting in promulgation of outlawry. The statute makes no distinction with respect to dangerousness. Nor is there any distinction based on the nature of the felony. One might expect that all accused murders or all accused rapists would be outlawed if they did not surrender and that lesser accused felons would not receive the status. If it is so, the record does not so indicate, and the statute itself makes no such distinction.[3] Whether one is outlawed appears to be a matter of caprice. At least ten of 30 district attorneys have never utilized the statute. The defendants suggest no standards that are used to determine whether an outlawry proceeding will be initiated against a fleeing felon, and the statute contains none.

The difference of treatment of the classes of accused felons is extreme. Since July 1, 1975, private persons may not make arrests in any situation, except when requested to provide assistance to law enforcement officers. N.C.G.S. 15A-404. And officers are authorized to use deadly force in arresting a person only when that person "presents an imminent threat of death or serious physical injury to others unless apprehended without delay..." N.C.G.S. 15A-401(d)(2).

Contrast the danger put upon the outlawed accused felon: if he should become fearful of armed citizens - not in uniform - and should run, he may be slain "without accusation of any crime." N.C.G.S. 15-48. The extreme remedy granted the citizenry infringes, we think, a fundamental right: that one not be denied life, or be wounded, except by due process of law.

[3] Whenever a statutory classification affects fundamental rights, it will encounter equal protection difficulties unless justified by a compelling governmental interest. *Shapiro v. Thompson*, 394 U.S. 618, 634, 638, 89 S.Ct. 1322, 22 L.Ed.2d 600 (1969); *Schilb v. Kuebel*, 404 U.S. 357, 365, 92 S.Ct. 479, 30 L.Ed.2d 502 (1971). We are inclined to think that the State's interest in the apprehension of one against whom an arrest warrant or indictment has been returned based on probable cause to believe that he has committed a capital felony, *e.g.*, murder, may properly be characterized as compelling. But that is not the thrust of the statute. The accused felon may be wholly innocent, and as we have discussed more fully under the preceding section, there is no requirement of a finding of probable cause to believe him guilty.

Moreover, felonies embrace a multitude of sins under the laws of North Carolina. In addition to capital felonies, it is provided by statute[4] that if the crime was a felony at common law it remains so under the law of North Carolina and that any offense punishable by imprisonment in the State's prison, even for a relatively short term, is a felony. Additionally, there are miscellaneous crimes that the legislature has seen fit to denominate as felonies. For example, if one of our college ball players should be accused of accepting or agreeing to accept a bribe given for the purpose of attempting to limit the margin of victory of his own team, he is guilty of a felony. N.C.G.S. 14-374. We doubt the legislature is fully aware that its statutory scheme has subjected college boys and girls to the risk of death at the hands of irate alumni if they fail to immediately surrender themselves to the local sheriff. We are quite certain that the State has no compelling interest that would justify licensing one's teammates to kill the pitcher if he should flee from them upon accusation of throwing the game or even cutting down the margin of victory. Without hesitation we hold that the State has failed to demonstrate a compelling

---

[3] Although Autry was accused of rape and other violent felonies, we note that when the dust settled in the criminal court, he was sentenced to 18 years' imprisonment for all offenses.

[4] N.C.G.S. 14-1.

governmental interest in the apprehension of *all* fleeing accused felons and that the statute as drawn and as administered violates the Equal Protection Clause of the Fourteenth Amendment.

[4,5] Even if we assume that the proper test is not "compelling interest," we come to the same conclusion. The traditional equal protection test is invidious discrimination. *Williamson v. Lee Optical*, 348 U.S. 483, 489, 75 S.Ct. 461, 99, L.Ed. 563 (1955). Sometimes it is denominated the "rational basis" test. *See McGowan v. Maryland*, 366 U.S. 420, 426, 81 S.Ct. 1101, 6 L.Ed.2d 393 (1961). "When the law lays an unequal hand on those who have committed . . . the same . . . offense . . ., it has made as invidious a discrimination as if it had selected a particular race or nationality for oppressive treatment." *Skinner v. Oklahoma*, 316 U.S. 535, 541, 62 S.Ct. 1110, 1113, 86 L.Ed. 1655 (1942). Some accused murders who fail to surrender are outlawed, and many others are not. To treat the same offenders differently is caprice and is irrational and violates the Equal Protection Clause.

The opposite is also true. It is irrational to treat a college boy accused of throwing a ball game the same as one accused of multiple homicides or bank robbery. It is also irrational, as applied, that a district attorney *or any other person* may occasion promulgation of outlawry against the college basketball player and leave one accused of a capital felony unscathed by the stringency of the statute. It is irrational that there are no standards either in the statute or in the course of the practice to guide prosecutors, not to mention mere citizens, in determining whether to seek promulgation of outlawry.

An appropriate judgment will be entered in accordance with this memorandum of decision adjudging N.C.G.S. 15-48 to be unconstitutional. Because we think a declaratory judgment will be sufficient relief for plaintiff and his class, we deny the prayer for injunctive relief.
420 F. Supp. 967 (E.D.N.C. 1976).

APPENDIX B

NEWSPAPER ARTICLES (EXCERPTED) COVERING BURGE'S DEATH

Newspaper articles reveal the insensitivity of the media in 1965 toward mentally ill people and racism.

THE SUN JOURNAL - MAY 12 1965
New Bern N.C.

Negro Gunman Terrorizes A Jones Highway

Couple Describes Events Of Recent Months To Reporter

By Randolph Thomas

According to a story Mr. and Mrs. Tommy Meadows unfolded in the office of Mrs. Eleanor Howard, U.S. Commissioner, a 260 pound Negro man, known as Wardell Burge, has declared this section, the Catfish Lake Road leading from Burge's home to N.C. Highway 58, "off limits to any and all persons."

Burge has also declared a Negro church in the area as "his pastorate." He frequently will take over the sermon by driving the preacher and congregation away.

Mrs. Meadows told of an incident ..."she and her three children were fired upon by the Negro while trying to start her husband's truck in a wooded area near her home." This incident provoked officers from Jones and Onslow County to arrest the Negro in 1963 and have him committed for a six month period in a mental institution... Burge was arrested...with law enforcement agents suffering two wounded and expending 16 tear gas pellets into the Negroe's home to no avail. They...succeeded in capturing him by trapping him in as upstairs room...and chopping the floor from under him. Leroy Trott...and an unidentified colored man were "cut" when Burge fell to the floor with knives in both hands.

THE SUN JOURNAL - MAY 13 1965
New Bern N.C.

Maysville Gunman Is Dead In Fire

MAYSVILLE, N.C. (AP) - An inquest will be held in the death of a former mental patient who burned while a posse was trying to arrest him.

Coroner George Davenport said the death of James Ordell [*sic*] Burge, 42, Wednesday was caused by asphyxiation, but an inquest will be held Monday.

Sheriff W.B. Yates said the 10-man posse was trying to arrest Burge on charges of assault with a deadly weapon.

Yates said Burge fired at them from an upstairs window and the 5 deputies used tear gas.

THE NEWS AND OBSERVER - May 15, 1965

Jones Man Defies Posse - Perishes in Fire

Maysville - A former mental patient died in a flaming upstairs room at his home Wednesday afternoon after firing wildly at District Solicitor Luther Hamilton of Morehead City and Deputy Warren Lanier of Onslow County.

Solicitor Hamilton, who ordered the arrest of Burgess [*sic*], had accompanied a posse to Burgess' [*sic*] home and "four or five shots" fired at Hamilton and Lanier missed their mark.

Officers hurled tear gas into the second story room...Sheriff Yates said. Before the gas cleared, the house caught fire inside...Yates said the fire was deliberately set.

KINSTON DAILY FREE PRESS-May 13, 1965

Jones County Man Dies in Fire While Resisting Law

Maysville (UPI) A coroner's inquest is scheduled here Monday in an effort to determine the cause of a fire which took the life of 41 year old James W. Burgess [*sic*], a former mental patient, late Wednesday.

The fire started after a posse ...hurled tear gas into the second story room...

Burgess [*sic*] refused the pleas of the officers when they tried to persuade him to surrender and fired wildly at District Solicitor Luther Hamilton Jr. and Deputy Sheriff Warren Lanier.

Sheriff W. B. Yates of Jones County said the fire was deliberately set.

THE JACKSONVILLE DAILY NEWS
Jacksonville, N. C.

Onslow Sheriff, Deputy
Hit By Shotgun Blasts

By Jim Robinson/Daily News Editor

...surrounding the home, an old

two-story building, and using police automobiles as protection, the officers attempted to convince Burges [*sic*] to give himself up. After repeated calls on the bull horn the former mental patient cut loose with his shot gun hitting Marshall and Lanier on the legs. No serious injury was received as the number seven shot was "pretty well spent." Three and possibly four shots were heard by officers before they attempted to shoot Burges [*sic*]. They tried to shoot for his legs.

Marshall and deputies filled the house with tear gas in attempts to force Burges [*sic*] to surrender.

Ernest Smith saw a curl of smoke and before anybody could do anything the entire house was completely covered with fire. The voluntary fire department was immediately called but the house was more than two-thirds gone by the time they arrived. Witnesses of the fire stated they had never seen anything burn so fast.

Jones County Sheriff Yates said the fire was deliberately set. Coroner George Davenport, of Jones County, said Burges's [*sic*] death was due to asphyxiation.

KINSTON DAILY FREE PRESS

Suicide

———

TRENTON (UPI) - A Jones County coroner's jury Monday night ruled suicide was the cause of death of James Burgess [*sic*] who suffocated in his blazing home while sheriff's deputies were trying to get him to lay down his gun and surrender on May 12th.